Echoes on the Bayou

Sins of Bear Corner
Book 1

By: Mary Reason Theriot

Echoes on the Bayou

Dedication

Without the love and support of my family and friends, I would not have pursued this new path in life. I would especially like to thank those that have proofread copy after copy, to give me their honest opinion of the books.

Theresa, thank you so much for your continued encouragement. Without you, some of the characters would not have "come to life."

To my wonderful husband Malwen, your continued love and support mean the world to me. I don't know what I would do without you in my life. One of these nights I'm sure you will be able to sleep with both eyes closed. Eventually I should run out of ideas... or maybe not. These books wouldn't be what they are without you pushing me forward.

To Yuri Theriot and Don Reason for all of your input.

To Don Reason and Malcolm "Phil" Theriot for sharing your knowledge and experience of law enforcement protocol.

To my fans, I would like to offer a special thank you for your continued support.

ISBN-10: 1-945393-10-6
ISBN-13: 978-1-945393-10-5

Also Available by Mary Reason Theriot:

The Hideaway

The Traveler

Dr. Frankenstein

Above Suspicion

Horror in the Night

Deadly Seduction

Seven Deadly Sins

A Kiss So Deadly

A Deadly Combination

www.maryreasontheriot.com

Prologue

Night had long since fallen. Not a star shone in the velvet sky. There was no moon to cast its warm glow. Darkness clutched the bayou in a grip as cold and black as death. Fog slithered among the cypress trunks like ghostly snakes.

Hiding in the dark, one with the night, he patiently watched the house. The wicked must be vanquished from this earth or they would lead more down the path to evil with their temptations.

One would fall prey tonight; one would be no more. One would pay for her sins.

The smell of her sin called to him, beckoning him forward. His soulless eyes sought out and found the one he deemed in need of saving. Shoulder length auburn hair and eyes the color of liquid chocolate bid a companion farewell.

She was the one. His hands clenched into fists, the sinewy muscles in his biceps grew taut. A lump rose in his throat.

He inhaled the night air to give him strength. Righteous eyes looked up and down the road to confirm that no one was around.

Only the sounds of the night filled the air. He slipped the gloves over his hands, turning the knob easily. No locks stopped him, proof that God's will was at work.

The dark soul slipped into her house. His muscles tensed in anticipation. The serrated knife tucked safely in his waistband gave him a sense of raw power. He anxiously waited to feel the cold steel blade slice through the soft womanly flesh, spilling her blood. Life and death lay in his hands.

Blood pulsed through his body, pounding in his ears. He could already smell the scent of her spilled blood.

A scream was cut short and soon a life would be no more.

It was his mission in life to rid the earth of these wretched women.

Chapter 1

Erica Devareaux walked home with nothing to illuminate the dark streets, but the dim streetlights. Although accustomed to going places by herself in the wee hours of the morning, she still had a feeling of trepidation raising the hairs on the back of her neck and goosebumps along her skin.   In a hurry to get to her car, Erica glanced both ways and then jogged across the intersection.

A light breeze lifted her brown hair away from her face and sent a chill down her spine. A cold certainty washed over her - she was being watched. Her gut clenched as she looked around.

A flicker of movement in the shadows startled her. Something in the alley moved. A shadow passed, darting to the other side. Her heart thumped wildly against her chest. She laughed when she saw an alley cat.

"There is nothing to fear but fear itself," she quoted into the still night air. If she continued repeating it to herself, then perhaps she would believe it.

Goosebumps still crawled over her body and the tightening of her muscles warned her not to let her guard down. Within minutes she would be safe in her car, heading back to her house. She grimaced at the way her life had turned out. She had been born into money, but when her father learned about her extracurricular activities, he disowned her.

Reaching the parking lot, Erica looked over the area. The first thing she learned out on the streets was to be aware of her surroundings at all times. She was thankful for the self-defense classes she had taken as a teenager.

Not a soul could be seen, though several cars were in the lot. Satisfied, Erica stuck her key in the lock and opened the door.

"Excuse me," came from behind her, causing her heart to jump into her throat. She heard the man chuckle, "I'm sorry, I didn't mean to scare you."

Erica looked at the tall man standing near her Chevy Cavalier. "You scared the hell out of me," she laughed nervously.

She looked him over more thoroughly. This good looking man stood well over six feet tall. His dirty blond hair and blue-gray eyes had to attract women easily.

"I was wondering if I could buy you breakfast."

Unaccustomed to that particular pick up line, she hesitated a moment before responding. "I'd like that."

His eyes gleamed in the obscure light. "My car is right over there. Why don't I drive us?"

"Okay." She relocked her car before heading off with him. She had planned on calling it a day, but money was money. She followed him through the parking lot to an older, weathered dark green Dodge truck that probably had not seen a car wash in years. He obviously didn't care about what he drove and she hoped he could pay for her services.

She wasn't into handing out freebies, no matter how good looking.

Being a true southern gentleman he unlocked her door, opened it and then walked around to his side of the truck to get in. She scooted closer to him, taking advantage of the bench seat.

"Do you want to do it right here or would you rather go somewhere private, sugar?" She asked as she used the rear view mirror to check her makeup.

"I know an out of the way spot down the road," he said. His eyes surveyed the parking lot before starting his truck.

She touched his forearm in an attempt to put him at ease, but he still flinched from her touch. "What's wrong?" she purred into his ear.

Instead of answering her, he stared into the night as he drove out of the parking lot.

***

He had been observing her every movement these last few days. She was a whore, pure and simple. This city was infested with the likes of her, a wanton woman. They expertly mastered the art of trickery with their deceiving words and seductive bodies. They corrupted the just and led them down a path full of sin. They were serpents who spoke with scheming tongues. They were pupils of Lucifer himself.

Human viciousness had jaded him into a cynic. He tried to keep his cynicism in check, but at times it landed him in trouble. Which might explain why he had so few friends.

Chapter 2

Living on the bayou was about survival, survival of the fittest to be exact. It was an instinctual response of fight to live. He wondered if she would fight back or if she would accept her fate with dignity.

As he headed out he observed his surroundings. Cypress trees dripping with Spanish moss outlined the brackish water of the bayou. The sun rose, silhouetting the horizon in a halo of light. The only noise outside was the incessant noise of the insects buzzing. The mosquitos were bad at this hour. Up ahead the red eyes of an alligator watched as he started the engines of the shrimp boat. Suddenly the gator's jaw snapped as it bit down on the fish in its mouth. Here in the bayou, he could watch as the cycle of life and death came full circle.

He headed down to the cabin to see if she was awake. He opened the door slowly. A smile formed across his face when he heard her moan. Soon he would set her free. First, she had to atone for her sins, the cheap whore.

****

It was the cold that woke her. It seeped into her bones, creeping along excruciatingly sensitive nerve endings. Her eyelids fluttered as she fought unconsciousness. The unbearable cold tempted her to sink back into the sweet abyss. She would have too, but her sluggish brain finally registered what her senses had been trying to tell her - she was covered in ice, submerged in it.

Panic shot through her when she realized how dark it was; she had always been deathly afraid of the dark. She tried to lurch to her feet, but her movements were restricted. She felt around and discovered that she was confined in a large box. She tried to clear her mind, to recall how she got here. She feared that she had been buried alive, and covered in ice. Unable to take the cold any longer, she slipped back into unconsciousness.

As she regained consciousness, she became aware of a throbbing pain that radiated throughout her body. She also had a violent, unrelenting headache.

She soon realized that she was now naked and secured to a table. Along her back, she could feel the splinters from the wood pricking her bare skin. Her wrists and ankles were bound with zip ties. She tried to breathe in, but it felt as if someone was sitting on her. When she looked up, she was staring into the eyes of her captor - a monster worse than she could ever imagine.

As his eyes roamed over her body, the mere thought of him touching her made her cringe. He scrutinized her face as if searching for something, for what she was not sure. She tried to convince herself this was a nightmare, one she would wake up from at any moment. But instead, she was looking into the eyes of the man who would set her soul free. Would God forgive her for everything she had done? Silently she begged God for His forgiveness.

He wrapped his hands around her throat and squeezed. Not enough to kill her, but enough to show her he was in control. Her eyes snapped open as she tried to move her head but his grasp on her was strong. She looked up at him in terror. "You will be cleansed of your sins tonight."

Her lungs were on fire, desperately needing air. Her skin mottled and turned purple as her eyes bulged.

"Sinner, are you ready to have your soul cleansed?"

What he said had her mortified; terrified of what he may do next.

He continued, "You must confess your sins to be absolved."

She tried to make sense of what he was saying. Panic surged through her body. An animal instinct and elemental will to survive took over. She pulled at the restraints as hard as she could, but her attempts were futile, the restraints were too tight. Fear ran in rivulets down her back. The presence of true evil was heavy in the air, as thick as the fog that hung over the bayou in the early morning hours.

His hands grabbed her neck, and his thumbs pressed against her windpipe. He had a wild look of rage in his eyes. She gasped for air as he squeezed tighter.

She knew from the sheer size of him, he could easily snap her neck. There was a madness to his technique, and he wasn't ready to kill her yet.

Right before she lost consciousness, he loosened his grip. It was as if he could sense she was getting ready to pass out.

She watched as he raised a hammer from nearby. This was it; this was how he would kill her. Time stood still as the hammer struck her shoulder. The excruciating pain caused her to release a guttural scream that pierced the night. The night air swallowed her scream, heard by no one.

She would not beg this man for mercy. It would only excite him and she refused to give him that satisfaction. She always knew that she would die young. She readily accepted this hand life had dealt her.

She had never endured such intense pain before. She prayed that the pain would become too much and allow her to drift off into unconsciousness, sparing herself any continued agony.

She swore his purpose in life was to torment her. He was playing a sick and twisted game. He paused, as if waiting for her to beg him to stop. Instead, she looked up at him with defiance in her eyes.

She wished she had led her life down a different path. When she died no one would remember her, no one would mourn her death. She had made too many poor choices in her life. She had no accomplishments, made no contributions to mankind. She would simply fade into oblivion. Would her body be found, or would it be as if she never existed?

As she lay waiting for his next punishment, she reminisced about her life. If only she could change the past. Maybe then she could alter the future, make better choices. If she had lived her life differently, would she be in bed with her husband instead of being tortured by this demented man?

She noticed a difference in his eyes, a determination in them. The corners of his mouth twitched into a hideous smile. She closed her eyes, unable to look at her captor's face anymore. She hoped that God was indeed merciful.

Her life was about to end in a most diabolical way. Fate had dealt her a cruel blow.

***

He had no pity for this sinner. He would have no second thoughts about killing her. She brought this upon herself by selling her body, tempting men. As her body shuddered, he released his grip on her. He couldn't kill her until she repented for her sins, she must ask for God's forgiveness.

Soon he would save her soul. He was halfway there, but first she had to confess. He needed to calm himself and prepare her body for cleansing. He would finish what God had asked him to do.

The control he had over her life made him feel alive. Soon, he would complete this mission and be with the woman he loved. He picked up the hammer and took another swing at her, striking her knee. He heard the bone splintering from the impact. "Are you ready to atone for your sins, harlot?"

When she did not answer, he raised the hammer again and hit her foot this time. Each blow slammed hard against her body, yet she still refused to ask for forgiveness. This one was stubborn.

The brutal force of each blow crushed and shattered her small bones. Blood sprayed him. He forced himself not to kill her. This was not how he wanted her to die.

But he had failed. She never asked for forgiveness. He prayed that as she died, she found God in her watery grave.

The fog rolled along the bayou, obscuring the moon. The mist swirled around him, hiding his secrets. He listened to make sure there were no other boats around him before bringing her topside. Darkness encased him. The wind tenderly blew through the trees. The quiet night prepared itself for her salvation.

As he cut the zip ties from her wrists and ankles, she did not fight. He picked her up and threw her over his shoulder, carrying her out to the deck of the boat.

As he stood over her, his hulking figure gawked at her face with a haunting penetration. He attached the shackles to her legs. The shackles were secured to the cement blocks. Once her legs were restrained, he kicked her body hard before he threw her into the murky water of the bayou.

"Sinner, it is time for your soul to be cleansed. You must find redemption."

Moonlight danced across the languid waves of the bayou. It was time for the finale. After he confirmed that she had made it to her grave, he proceeded down the bayou. If he didn't return with any shrimp people would wonder why he had stayed out for so long.

***

The coolness of the water woke her. It took her a moment to realize she was free. That feeling was fleetingly brief as she heard the loud splash of the blocks hit the water. The further down she sank, the harder it became to hold her breath. She would drown to death in this murky water. No one would find her body. This would be where she spent eternity. As the blocks sank to the bottom of the bayou, she let out one last breath and again, she prayed that God would have mercy on her soul.

Chapter 3

Mia Arnold could not remember the last time she had a good night's sleep. Her body ached from the sheer exhaustion of her busy life. Business was picking up at the bakery. They had several cake orders to fill just for that weekend alone.

She also had the annual Multiple Sclerosis fundraiser coming up and needed to prepare for that. Even though she had moved away from New Orleans, she promised the council that she would stay active with the fundraiser. However, she had been so busy starting her business in Bear Creek that she forgot to arrange the fundraiser. Thankfully, she still had a month to prepare. She needed to call The Riverside Inn and confirm they could use the banquet room again this year. Lately, she felt as if she was being pulled in twenty different directions.

Once she pulled into her drive she began to relax, everything had a way of working out. Everything would fall into place.

She loved her quaint house. The bayou was in her backyard and the bakery was ten minutes away. Bear Corner had grown substantially over the years. Her parents were euphoric that she moved back home. As much as she loved New Orleans, when she came home late one night to find someone in her apartment she decided to move. She didn't want to become one of the many casualties there.

Mia had managed to save a good sum of money working for one of the top restaurants in New Orleans. Since she worked almost twenty-four/seven and didn't have much of a life, she never had time to spend her money.

As soon as she saw the weathered building that housed her bakery, she knew it would be perfect. Located on the corner of Main and Jackson, the bakery overlooked the bayou. The kitchen was off to one side of the building which allowed the dining room a view of the bayou. It had once been an elegant restaurant that failed due to poor management. The location was perfect for a business. The old building still held its original embossed white tin ceilings reminiscent of the era in which it was built. While cleaning out a storage closet in the back of the kitchen, she found an antique cash register. After a thorough cleaning, it now sat proudly on top of one of the glass display cases. Their actual cash register was hidden in a cabinet behind it. She arranged several glass display cases near the kitchen so when they exited the kitchen with the treats they could arrange them right in the case. The setup also helped to keep the flow of the main area pleasant and open. Guests could sit at the small bistro tables and enjoy the scenery.

Unlocking the front door of her house, she walked inside and breathed a sigh of relief. Out of habit she walked around the house to ensure that no intruders were lurking about. This was a habit she had had ever since that fateful day. She even slept with a nightlight. She had become paranoid, even though she should feel safer here than in New Orleans.

When she decided to move back home, Mia's parents suggested that she live with them, but she needed her space. As much as she loved them, she could not keep her sanity living with her parents. Besides, when she stepped into this house she fell in love with it. It may be bigger than a single person needed, but the house had her dream kitchen. It was large, spacious and had almost every amenity someone like her could want. The kitchen, dining room and living room were one great room that overlooked the bayou. There were two small bedrooms along with a roomy master bedroom. Mia turned one of the bedrooms into a spare room and the other into her office. The screened in back porch had a magnificent outdoor kitchen installed by the previous owner, which allowed her to either cook indoors or out. It was as if this house had been designed for her.

The house was the perfect setup for her. When she wasn't at the bakery she was here working on new recipes. One of these days Mia hoped to write a cookbook. Right now, she was happy playing around in the kitchen.

She walked into her bathroom and opened the door of the large walk in shower. Reaching in, she turned the porcelain knobs to just the right temperature of water. As she undressed, she looked around at the gorgeous Italian marble tile, double vanity and the jetted tub. What a change from the small bathroom in her old apartment.

By the time she had finished, it was almost midnight. Climbing underneath the covers, she pushed all other thoughts from her mind. She fell asleep within minutes. Tomorrow would be another hectic day, and she needed the rest.

***

He watched her house from the bayou. He had been working diligently to rid the streets of New Orleans of sinners, but what did he do now that she had moved back home? Was God telling him it was time to rid Bear Corner of its sinners too?

He still couldn't believe God had brought her back to him. But first he must finish doing God's bidding. There were too many more souls to cleanse before he could make her his. Everything had to be perfect, and the world was still far from perfect.

The love he felt for her had grown stronger over the years. He knew, in time, she would feel the same way for him. He must wait for the perfect moment to let her know of his unrequited love.

Whispering to her house, "I won't keep you waiting much longer. Soon we will be together and so happy. You will love me even more when I tell you everything I have done for you. Sweet dreams my love."

Chapter 4

As he walked the streets of New Orleans, he realized how much temptation there was here. Sinners surrounded him. By his own pathetic admission, he recognized the weakness of man and had no desire to turn to Satan. His mother's warnings of sins of the flesh echoed through his mind.

He studied her with mean, hardened eyes. He knew her schedule. She had no idea he had been watching her, learning the best time to strike.

She left for work at the same time, worked the same corner. Night in and night out she followed the same routine. It was easy to figure her out. He made sure that she was a sinner beforehand. Only those that needed to be cleansed would be saved by him.

***

The hairs on the back of her neck rose, and a sudden intense feeling of being watched washed over her. She turned around and scanned the restaurant, rubbing the goose bumps from her arms. The uneasiness did not abate.

She picked up her remaining food and dumped it in the trash can. As she left the restaurant, she took a final look around to see if someone was watching her. There in a far corner of the restaurant she noticed a man dressed in black staring at her. She couldn't make out his face since he had a baseball cap pulled down low over his head. As he waved, she realized he wasn't staring at her, but someone else standing behind her.

Chalking it up to a case of shot nerves, she tried to ignore the unsettled feeling. A shudder ran down her spine as she exited the restaurant. She had spooked herself this time.

When a slight noise caught her attention, she stopped walking and turned around. She was certain she'd heard heavy footsteps behind her. Perhaps it was a lonely man seeking comfort from one of them. She picked up her pace, not wanting another girl to take her spot. The quicker she walked, the faster the footsteps echoed behind her. She became scared when it sounded like the footsteps were getting closer. Panicking, she looked around one more time to make sure she wasn't being followed.

When she didn't see anyone, she took a deep breath and forced herself to relax. She had made it to her corner. None of the other girls were here; maybe they had found "dates".

Then she heard another sound, as if feet were shuffling along the sidewalk. The closeness of it disturbed her. She looked around and again saw nothing. Wait, there in the shadows along the alley something moved, but it was only a blur.

Then the pain hit her. Something heavy struck her temple. She remembered seeing a flash of light before losing consciousness.

✱✱✱

He watched as she left the restaurant and followed her as she walked back to her usual corner. The streets in this area were poorly lit, helping to hide his movements. Her blond wig stood out among the other girls making her easy to follow. As he took a deep breath in, he could smell her perfume that clung to the air.

After knocking her unconscious, he loaded her into the cab of his truck and restrained her. He covered her with a blanket, keeping her out of sight. Making sure the area was still empty, he pulled away. Once they were at the boat, he placed her in a large ice chest and covered her with ice. Tonight he would move her to his workroom.

He started the engines of the shrimp boat and headed straight for the horizon, anxiously waiting for when he could save her soul.

Now that darkness had fallen and no one was around, he moved her into the small cabin. As he undressed her, the sight of her breasts stirred a desire deep inside of him. He forced himself to look away. He must not give in to temptation. She was a sinner, not to be touched. Yet it was difficult when their bodies were so alluring.

***

It was the cold that first woke her. It settled deep in her bones and sent agonizing pain through her body. Her eyelids fluttered as she fought to stay awake.

Panic shot through her when she realized someone had submerged her in ice. She was in a large box, possibly an ice chest. She tried to recall how she'd gotten here, but, unable to take the cold any longer, she slipped back into unconsciousness.

When she regained consciousness, she couldn't move her arms or legs. She looked up at her captor and a chill swept through her body, "You are a sinner and must find redemption."

"You son of a bitch, how dare you judge me!"

He looked down at her with contempt in his eyes, "I am not your judge, only God is."

She wondered what this monster had planned for her. By the swaying of the room, she assumed she was on a boat and, judging from the smell, she figured it was a shrimp boat.

He glared at her. His eyes were fierce, almost savage, and filled with pure hatred. He narrowed them as he looked at her. He had a hard face, bleak and bitter. Anger permeated every inch of his expression. She was stunned by the seething intensity of his fury. She didn't even know this man.

She cried, trying to erase the images of things he could do to her from her mind. No matter how hard she tried, she couldn't stop the visions running through her mind. Her blood began to curdle. This would end very badly for her and in the worst possible way. She had no doubt her captor would be cold blooded and unmercifully cruel. With this sudden realization, she did something she hadn't done in a long time, she begged God for forgiveness and mercy.

Suddenly, he slapped her hard. The force was harder than she expected, and she tasted blood from where she bit her tongue. She stared up at him and swore that she was looking at true evil. More pain coursed through her when he took the hammer and swung it. She heard bone breaking as the hammer made an impact with her hand. She yelled out as the piercing pain became all consuming. All she could do was lie there motionless, broken, jagged and in pain.

As he prepared to strike her again with the hammer, she drew in a deep breath. A deathly calm wrapped itself around her soul. She braced herself for another impact. She clamped her teeth against the scream that would erupt. She bit down so hard she tasted more blood. She must have bitten down on her tongue again.

Her cries of mercy went unheard. She prayed for a means to escape or a savior, someone to rescue her before she was violently murdered. Instead, she was forced to endure more pain.

***

The fear frozen on her face stirred something inside of him. He reached down and stroked one of her breasts. He knew it was wrong, but touching her young, firm body became too much temptation for him. Darkness surrounded them; no one could see what he was doing. All he saw was emptiness. He prayed for divine intervention. He did not want to give into temptation.

He saw her eyes flicker for a moment and waited for her vision to come back into focus. As he towered over her, he asked, "Are you ready to be freed, sinner?"

He preferred to talk to his victims, make them understand the importance of his work. He wanted them to understand why he was doing this. They must accept their fate and accept his gift of salvation.

She spat at him, "I don't need to be saved." She muttered.

He looked down at her as she lay on the table. Her slender arms and legs still secured to the table. She was near death and almost ready to be set free. The decision of when to release her soul was his mission. She must atone for her sins to be saved.

As pools of blood formed on the floor from her injuries, her life slowly ebbed from her body. She would soon be cleansed in the muddy waters of the bayou.

Chapter 5

The cool air felt good. Too bad it wouldn't stay that way.
By afternoon, the heat of the sun combined with the
humidity would have it feeling like a sauna. By the end of
the month, May would be hot and muggy, which was typical
of Louisiana weather.

He threw her overboard like a fisherman would toss a net.
Her body flew effortlessly over the edge of the boat. She
was semi-conscious, barely breathing. She thudded loudly
against the surface of the water. He could picture the water
flowing over her body, cradling her, before swallowing her
whole.

He wished it wasn't so dark and he could watch as she sunk
to the bottom of the bayou. But he couldn't take the
chance of turning on his running lights. If he could only do
this during the daylight, but too many people were out on
the water during the day. He couldn't take the chance of
someone passing by and getting curious as to what he was
doing, why he wasn't casting his nets yet. Someone may
worry that he was broken down and stop to offer him
assistance.

As he threw the concrete blocks overboard he would set her
soul free. She could no longer tempt men with that luscious
body of hers. This would be her final baptism, asking God to
forgive her sins. The bayou waters would help cleanse her
soul, making sure she was welcomed into the Kingdom of
God.

She would no longer suffer or fear anything ever again. The lulling of the water would calm her nerves as she died. It would suck her into its depths, burying her in its murky waters forever. He weighed the bodies down to prevent them from floating to the surface. He could not be found out until his mission here on earth was complete.

Fatigue set in. Freeing these poor lost souls seemed to take everything out of him. Unfortunately, he had no time to go home. He still had to cast his shrimp nets and bring home a catch. People would become curious if he came home empty handed and the other shrimpers had caught their fill.

It was time to move on. There was still so much work to do, still so many sinners to cleanse. There was no one else to do his work. Who else would do God's bidding?

Chapter 6

Mia heard her alarm clock going off and wanted to hit the snooze button, but knew she couldn't. She had to get to the bakery early this morning and help Shelly, her assistant, prepare the beignets and other goodies for the morning crowd. She had always been an early riser and didn't think opening at six o'clock in the morning would be too difficult. However, she never expected the bakery to be a success so early on. By six o'clock they had a line forming out front and some days by eight o'clock they were sold out.

After a month of being open, she was getting into a routine, and everything seemed to be running smoother. Her kolache dough could be used for the kolaches and the cinnamon rolls. Most of the doughs she used could be prepared the day ahead and kept in the massive refrigerator.

The only items that had to be made to order were the muffin and cake batter. Even the cookie batter could be prepared ahead of time. Currently, her biggest sellers were the beignets and café au laits. Mon deiu, and, of course, her cakes brought in a nice profit. Thankfully, she had the mindset to let people preorder. Even though the shop closed at one o'clock in the afternoon, she and Shelly stayed late to fill the orders. If this kept up, she wouldn't have any problem making her house or business note. She was glad she took the risk and opened a bakery here. The town didn't need another restaurant, and it would have been a tough market to break into. However, when moving here, she noticed that there was not a place for breakfast goodies or cakes, other than the local grocery store. She saw a potential business opportunity and went for it – now it was paying off.

Mia haphazardly threw on a pair of jeans and T-shirt and took a quick glance at herself in the mirror. She was losing weight. She had been so busy that she hadn't had a chance to sample the treats she baked, which was a good thing. After getting dressed, she walked into the kitchen. The coffee was almost done brewing. Before leaving, she cooked a bagel sandwich with egg whites and turkey sausage for breakfast. If today was as busy as yesterday, she doubted she would stop until sometime after lunch and needed something to hold her up. She had been considering adding a variety of breakfast sandwiches and individual quiches to the menu, but she wanted a solid routine in place before adding more items to the menu.

Once things calmed down she would get into a better routine of eating and spend more time focusing on her. Maybe after the charity function she should consider taking off for a few days. Shelly and her mother could handle the bakery for a few days. Just thinking about a vacation helped put her mind at ease. She could spend a few days at the beach and soak up the sun.

Mia grabbed the mail on her way out. When she had a chance, she would go through it and see which bills had to be paid right away. At least there wasn't too much piled up in the mailbox. She placed everything on the passenger seat and headed to the bakery.

It was after lunch before she had an opportunity to go through the mail. Most of it was junk mail. She set the bills aside to pay from her home computer later that night. Among the stack of mail was a small padded envelope. She checked the return address, but couldn't find one. *Strange there's no postage on the envelope either.* Inside was a small jewelry sized box containing a single stud earring. She wondered who sent this to her. Maybe it was someone's idea of a weird welcome home gift. She put everything back in the envelope and stuffed it into her desk drawer.

She looked up from her desk to find her mother standing in the doorway. "I brought you lunch. I figured you didn't take a break to eat."

Getting up from her desk, she gave her mom a kiss on her cheek, "Thanks so much, Mom. This is perfect. I am starving."

Her mother told her, "Sit, eat. You need to take better care of yourself. You look overworked."

"It's getting better, I promise. Everything is falling into a routine now."

She asked, "Is there anything I can help you with?"

"Not really. I have the MS function I still need to put together and after that I may have you watch over the bakery for a day or two. I was thinking of slipping away to the beach for a few days."

"Well of course I will. You need a vacation."

Her mom asked, "How is the fundraiser coming?"

"I need to contact the hotel to see if they will offer the same deal as they did last year. I also want to contact the local restaurants to see if this year they would consider offering a sample menu free of charge."

Her mom looked surprised, "Do you think you can get them to agree to this?"

"It's worth a chance. I'm going to stress the free publicity their generous donation will be getting."

She smiled at her daughter, "I guess it's worth a try. Let me know if there is anything I can do to help."

After her mom had left, Mia went back into the kitchen and started preparing the dough for the next day.

Chapter 7

A chill ran down her spine as she spotted the open window. She shouldn't be so careless. A howling wind caused branches of the large oak tree on the side of her room to scratch the bedroom window. A storm must be blowing in. She made it home just in time.

Weather in Louisiana had always been capricious. A perfect afternoon could yield a thunderstorm by evening. Rain showers could become horrendous downpours in the blink of an eye.

The air was thick with the coming of summer; sweat dampened her skin. The dank smell of the slow moving river invaded the room from the open window. She could hear the hum of the traffic, a steady rush that drowned out the other sounds of the city. She walked over to the window, closing it and making sure that it was locked.

For a fleeting moment, a feeling of impending evil pierced her mind. Her blood chilled with the looming dark thought.

Once she secured the window, she made her way to the bathroom. She needed to shake this uneasy feeling and went to run her bath water before undressing. A hot bubble bath would help calm her nerves. She refused to give in to her fears and allow herself to jump at every shadow. She was safe in her small room.

She finished undressing and stepped into the tub, letting the bubbles caress her body. She was ready to climb into bed with a good book and forget this night ever happened.

With more working girls on the streets at night, it was becoming more difficult to earn a living.

The bathroom was nice and steamy from the hot water in the tub, reminding her of the fog that rolled in from the mighty Mississippi River. When the water began to cool, she stepped out of the tub. Grabbing a towel, she wrapped it around her body, wiped the steam off the mirror and stared at her reflection. The years on the streets were taking a toll on her body. The meth had stained her teeth. She couldn't believe that this was what had become of her life.

Slipping on a pair of sweats, she turned off the bathroom light and headed back into her bedroom. The hotel room wasn't much, but the rent was cheap and she didn't have to share it with anyone else. She'd found a romance book in the trash can today, and it caught her attention. This was a luxury for her; she could rarely afford a book to read. Tonight she would lose herself in the book, dreaming that she was the woman being made passionate love to and not some john wanting to find a quick release.

She climbed into bed and pulled the quilt over her, making sure she was nice and snug. Reaching under the mattress, she made sure her security blanket was still safe and sound. She had cut out a small hole underneath the bed and stuffed a wallet in there with her life's savings. She had saved up a couple of grand, and soon she could move away from here. She planned on catching a bus to Lafayette and starting a new life, something that didn't involve spreading her legs for men. She figured she needed a few hundred more to get a hotel room there and find a job. She had learned to live cheap, so that was not a problem. The streets were getting dangerous. It was time to move on. When she left, she wouldn't look back.

She knew she could ask her sister for help, but she didn't want to disappoint her. After all, her sister was a successful business woman and might not take the news well that she was a street walker and a drug addict.

Not long after she had fallen asleep, something jolted her awake. He pounced before she could react. He was too strong to fight him. His nails dug into her face as he forced her to breathe in the ether soaked rag. Her body weakened fast. Everything became hazy as she succumbed to the drug.

She woke up freezing. She was not sure which was worse, the bitter cold or the terror that paralyzed her body. It all came back to her at once, the intruder overpowering her in her room. She felt around, trying to ascertain where she was. She feared that someone had her submerged naked in ice. Her skin was covered in goosebumps, and her teeth couldn't stop chattering from the cold. She tried to see through the darkness that enveloped her. The cold seeped deep into her bones, the pain became all consuming. Once again, she slipped into darkness.

When her eyes fluttered open, she was in a different place. She tried to move her arms and legs, but someone had restrained her to a table. Terror washed over her body. Who could have done this? What did he have planned for her? The swaying of the room made her nauseous. The movement reminded her of being on a boat. She wished she had taken heed to the rumors. The rumble of the engines confirmed that she was on a boat.

She observed her surroundings, hoping to find a means of escape. She heard someone coming, and fear washed over her as her captor came into view, only it was too dark to make out his face.

He grabbed a fist full of her hair and forced her to look at him, "Please, if you let me go I won't tell anyone. I swear!"

He studied her face for a moment and then let go of her. Looking into his eyes sent a shiver down her spine. His eyes were soulless, devoid of life. "I cannot free you until you are saved."

As he groped her breasts, she cringed. She wished she could slap his hand away. Tears streamed down her face as she wondered what he planned to do to her. She hollered out, "Help! Somebody please help me."

He sneered at her, "No one can hear you out here. I chose this place because you need to be cleansed. You are a sinner."

She could not come to terms with what was happening. It had to be a nightmare.

"I'm not a sinner. I promise you." He reared back and slapped her hard across the face. She immediately tasted blood. Pain and terror gripped her body.

"Liar! I have watched you. I know what you do."

She swallowed hard, hoping to force the terror back down. She pulled at the restraints one more time, but he had made sure she was tightly secured. She was his prisoner, and there was no way to escape.

She watched his facial expressions change as he picked up the hammer and waved it in the air. It appeared that evil had consumed him all at once.

She feared her life would come to an end by the hands of her captor. At any time, this could be her last breath. She felt the hammer come down on her knee with a deadly thud. She prayed death came fast. The pain was excruciating, and she wasn't sure how much more of this torture she could take. She had no idea the human body held so much blood. Her blood coated the walls.

As her body grew weaker, he asked, "Are you ready to confess your sins to Almighty God?"

She let out a chilling scream that became lost in the night. "Oh please, why, oh why won't you just let me die?"

"Not until you ask God for forgiveness."

After all the pain she had endured, she was ready to do anything to make this end. "Please forgive me for my sins? I am truly sorry."

As he hoisted her onto his shoulder, and carried her onto the deck of the boat, the night air clung to her bare skin. She was grateful to be out of that room. It was pitch black out here except for the soft glow of the moon. She wondered what he had planned for her next. He had tortured her, but never once did he rape her. He kept talking about cleansing and salvation.

****

God's mission for these sinners helped him find an inner peace. His skin tingled and his pulse raced as he thought of the next soul he would save. It was God's will, and he would not disappoint Him. As he performed God's will, he remained calm, knowing he was saving this world from another evil temptation. No sweaty palms or jittery feelings would keep him from performing his task at hand.

Tranquility came over him as she asked for forgiveness. His mission was almost complete. She must be cleansed. He was mentally and physically exhausted, but he still had a lot to do before he could crawl into bed.

Alone at the helm, he headed out during the predawn darkness. He listened to the soft rush of water as *Marie II* cut through the bayou water on its way to the Gulf of Mexico. Guided strictly by instinct, he headed out to complete God's mission.

Beyond the dim glow of the instrument panels, the boat ran dark. Not even running lights revealed his location.

The air hung heavy with a humidity that clung to him. There was a chance of thunderstorms this afternoon.

He aimed a flashlight into the blackness of the night and confirmed that no one else was out there. He turned off the flashlight and let the darkness envelop him once again. Dawn was fast approaching, and he must cleanse her before daybreak.

This was the time of day he preferred the most. Here he was miles from shore, surrounded by emptiness while the rest of the world slept.   This was where he felt closest to God.

He had learned from experience some sinners refused to confess to their sins, even after having pain inflicted on them.   It was a slow and tedious process. He didn't want them to die before begging God for forgiveness.

He tossed her overboard. Her body splashed loudly as it hit the murky water. As she thrashed about against the surface of the water, he threw the cinder blocks overboard to send her to her watery grave. He closed his eyes and imagined the water embracing her before swallowing her whole.

He said a novena as he set her soul free. She could no longer tempt men into committing such atrocious sins. This would be her final baptism. God would be able to forgive her for all of her sins. The bayou waters would cleanse her soul, allowing her entry into the Kingdom of God.

Chapter 8

He stepped into the night, his eyes focusing through the darkness. He breathed in the heady scent of the dark, insidious aroma of the bayou. The scents and hot breeze across his face transported him back in time.

He saw himself as a child playing in the swampland that bordered his parents' property. This was his escape from his dad. Here he could be anything he wanted. There were no expectations of what he should be doing, how he didn't compare to his dad at that age.

Even though his parents lived in the same town, he rarely saw his dad. There was no love lost between them. He suspected that ornery Cajun would be around for a while yet. He was too mean to die. He forced those memories back down. Now was not the time to dwell on things that he could not change. He had a mission to complete.

Even though he was engulfed in the darkness of the night, he swore she was looking directly at him. His black, glittering eyes watched her every movement. A feral hunger moved through him.

As he watched the woman who needed to atone for her sins, he ran the tip of the blade against his tongue, drawing blood. The metallic flavor fueled his desire and quickened his movements. He was ready to complete his mission so that he could be with his true love.

She was a dirty, filthy slut, and he had to teach her that her sins had consequences.

***

As she stared out into the night, she swore she felt the presence of evil beckoning her into the shadows of the night. A deep, primitive fear washed over her body, and she tried to shake off the eerie feeling.

Even though she was safe in her hotel room, she felt exposed. As if someone or something was watching her every move. With an uneasy knot in the pit of her stomach, she made sure all the doors and windows were locked.

Falling into a deep sleep, she woke up with a start, bolting upright. She didn't remember leaving the radio on and reached over to turn it off. A light breeze blew from the pedestal fan she bought for the room. She glanced around the room in a panic, trying to see what could have woken her. The light from the hall filtered through the doorway, illuminating the room softly.

Suddenly, the intruder grabbed hold of her and covered her nose and mouth with the rag. He was impossibly strong; his nails dug into her flesh while stopping her flailing. Whatever he had on the rag weakened her fast and the fight to survive left her body as everything went hazy. Her eyelids became heavy as she succumbed to the drug.

The cold woke her. She reached for her blanket, but instead grabbed air. Fear washed over her as confusion flooded her mind. She forced her eyes open, but all she saw was darkness. It was too dark to see where she was. She felt around, but all she felt was ice.

She was chilled to the bone. Darkness surrounded her. The cold was excruciating. Once again, she fell into unconsciousness.

As her eyes fluttered open, she realized she was no longer submerged in ice water. She tried to move her arms and legs, but someone had restrained her to a table. Terror paralyzed her body. Who could have done this to her and why? The room swayed back and forth in a gentle rocking motion. When she heard the rumble of the engines, she knew that she was on a boat. From the nauseating smell, it was probably a shrimp boat.

From the darkness, a voice called out, "You must atone for your sins."

She whimpered and struggled against the restraints. He had her wrists and ankles secured tightly. There was no chance of escaping.

"Please let me go," she sobbed. "I won't tell anyone what you did. Please, you don't have to hurt me."

He had taken her in the middle of the night. She couldn't remember his face, but there was no doubt he had drugged her. It was too dark to make out his facial features. She didn't know what he meant by atoning for her sins? Was he a religious freak that believed he could save her soul?

She pulled against the restraints again, and he laughed hard at her futile attempts. She cringed as he ran the knife over her naked body.

"Please I'm begging you," she implored, "let me go. I swear I won't tell anybody."

He chuckled as the knife cut into her body. White hot pain seared through her as tears blurred her vision. Her reaction was instantaneous, and she squirmed, trying to free herself.

"Please stop hurting me," she wailed as the excruciating pain consumed her.

She cried out in agony as the knife cut into her once again. She writhed against the restraints, but he didn't stop the torment. He slashed her repeatedly. Everywhere she looked she saw crimson smears. Blood seemed to drip from the ceiling.

She begged God for forgiveness, praying for death to come. Was he right, that her sins brought this on? She should have listened to Sister Teresa and kept herself pure.

His words echoed in her mind as she stared at the accusing finger coated in her blood. There were so many stab wounds, most shallow. At first the wounds were meant to be painful, but not fatal. This man had so much rage and hate inside of him.

She heard a whimper in the background and wondered who else could be witnessing this massacre. Then she realized that the sound was emitted from her throat, from deep inside of her. A primitive horror had taken over her body.

This was her fault. She did this to herself. If only she hadn't sinned. She closed her eyes, not wanting to see the blood, the rage, and the hate. Finally, silence washed over her; the pain no longer existed. She couldn't see the bloody hands reaching for her, freeing her from her restraints. She didn't feel him lifting her off of the table or see his eyes filled with condemnation.

***

He brought her almost lifeless body topside. It was pitch black except for the soft glow of the moon rolling over the waves. It was time for her final step of salvation.

He tossed her overboard and into the murky water with complete ease. She was near death as the water swallowed her whole. As he threw the concrete blocks overboard, he said a novena for her soul. The bayou waters would release her soul. Now that she was cleansed, she would be welcomed into the Kingdom of God.

Chapter 9

Shelly walked into the kitchen and asked, "Mia, can you come give me a hand? It is getting busy out here."

Detective Chad Picou saw her as soon as she walked into the room. Her long auburn hair cascaded past her shoulders, almost to the middle of her back. Her outfit clung to her in all the right places, showing every womanly curve of her body. She was more than a woman; she was the most beautiful woman he had ever laid eyes on. Her rich brown eyes had him intrigued; making his heart beat faster just looking at her.

Seeing her made him feel things he hadn't felt in a long time. He wondered if she knew just how stunning she was and how she captured the attention of every man she came into contact with.

She was extremely busy and now wasn't the time to introduce himself. There would be a better time; after all she was his next door neighbor.

***

Mia looked around the store and was surprised at how busy they were at this hour. She needed to make more dough this afternoon since business was increasing.

A man sitting in the back corner table caught her eye. He was a big, rugged looking man with dark brown hair. He looked a little older than her, but it was difficult to tell. She could tell by the color of his weathered skin he worked out in the sun, most likely a shrimper or oil rig worker, possibly both. He had the body of an athlete, broad shoulders and large hands. It felt as if he was staring right through her with his piercing eyes. When he saw her looking his way, he got up and left hastily. *That's odd, maybe he was shy.* Something about him looked vaguely familiar to her.

Mia prided herself on her keen awareness of details and her impeccable memory. As one of the top chefs in New Orleans, she learned right away to remember people's faces and always tried to remember their names. She didn't like to upset her customers when she couldn't place their face. There was something familiar about him, but she could not recall where she knew him from.

Normally she would shrug it off, but for reasons she couldn't fathom, it disturbed her that she couldn't remember him.

Chapter 10

He couldn't resist going into Mia's bakery to catch a glimpse of her. She beckoned him to her by some visceral connection that he could not explain. Since she arrived back in town, he had made sure not to contact her in case she recognized him. He wasn't ready for her to remember just yet, but soon it would be time. The impending moment when he stepped back into her life brought him great exhilaration. He hoped God would be merciful and bring Mia to him soon.

He sat back in his chair to drink a café au lait and snack on some beignets. As he looked around, he noticed that Mia was doing very well for herself here. The bakery was crowded and noisy, buzzing with activity. Maybe moving back home was for the best.

He watched as several people he knew came in and out. Whenever he recognized someone he brought the newspaper up to his face, not wanting to make small talk. He only came here to observe his Mia.

He enjoyed people watching. It was an enlightening hobby. Observing various human behaviors was an adventure. It was also an integral part of God's mission. He must make sure the person was a sinner so that their soul could be cleansed.

Earlier, he had observed a young girl come into the bakery. She was hanging all over an older man. She was a stunning young lady, but obviously a trollop. She wore a tight pair of jeans that looked as if they were painted on and a see through blouse that left nothing to the imagination. Her black lace bra could be seen through the shirt. Her perky boobs bounced with every giggle. He bet those were store bought, they didn't go with her body type.

At first he assumed they were father and daughter, until she kissed him on the mouth. The man must be a sugar daddy. Why else would an attractive woman be with someone who more than likely needed a string on his pecker just to find it. There was no doubt they were tourists. She was a bubbly blonde with an annoyingly loud giggle that he heard from where he sat in the back.

Since she may be his next victim, he needed to follow her and see if her soul had to be cleansed. Sinners should not be allowed to walk into his Mia's store. This young girl's soul must be purified.

Just the thought of this whore being near his Mia sent a menacing rage churning through him. He could visualize the sins that this young girl committed with this man. She was a slut, a harlot and shall be saved.

He reminded himself to get his rage under control; now was not the time to be careless. He still had more souls to cleanse and could not be stopped until he completed his mission.

He followed the trollop and her boyfriend out of the bakery. He couldn't believe his luck when they brought the food to their cabin. Now to wait and see if she snuck out while the old man slept.

***

Amber didn't think Douglas would ever fall asleep. It must have something to do with the air here. Usually he took an afternoon nap and was back in bed by eight o'clock sharp, not today, though. He had it in his mind that they should spend as much time as possible together before he had to return to real life tomorrow. If it weren't for the fact that he bought her whatever she wanted as well as the money, car and apartment she would dump him.

It took her a while to get accustomed to having sex with an older man, but at least he was what she would consider a minute man. The money made what little time she did endure with him worthwhile.

She snuck out of the cabin and headed down the stairs. Earlier she had noticed a bar not far from here that looked as if it could be a fun place. She might even find her a little something to play with on the side.

She never heard the man come up from behind her. She just felt his powerful arms wrap around her torso and restrain her arms. Before she could scream, he covered her mouth with a damp cloth and pressed it firmly against her mouth and nostrils. He forced her to breathe in the sweet smell of whatever he had on the rag.

She desperately fought to break free, trying to kick him, but she could not loosen the grip he had on her. The vapors from the ether soaked rag burned her throat and lungs, making her woozy. The world spun as her strength left her body. Her body felt like it belonged to a rag doll. She felt herself collapsing. She had sworn before she lost consciousness that she saw the face of the devil.

When Amber woke up, she felt disoriented, almost as if she was floating around the room. She must have turned the air conditioning down real low last night. She was freezing. As she went to reach for the covers, panic consumed her. She couldn't move her arms.

She had no immediate recollection of what happened. It took some time for her mind to clear. She had no concept of time. She tried to look around to see where she was, but it was too dark to make anything out.

Whatever her abductor used to knock her out had made her sick to her stomach, and the fishy smell in the room did not help matters. Her head felt as if it would split wide open.

What kind of twisted individual abducted a person in the middle of the night? The obvious conclusion frightened her. A shiver snaked down her spine. Why did she have to leave the room? She could have taken a sleeping pill and partied when she got back home.

In spite of feeling disoriented and sick to her stomach, she told herself to pull it together. She needed to keep her wits about her. Panicking now would do her no good. She was streetwise and could figure a way out of this mess. She needed to assess the situation and come up with a plan of attack. She enlisted every ounce of strength she could muster to suppress her fear and concentrated on surviving this ordeal. She did not want to die a grisly death. She pulled at the restraints harder hoping to break free, but her attempts were futile. The restraints refused to budge.

As she heard footsteps come closer, wild images of what her captor could do to her flashed through her mind.

A cold dread came across her when she heard him ask, "Are you ready to atone for your sins?"

She wondered what this maniac was talking about. How long had she been here? She knew one thing, time stopped and she was in hell.

As she zoned out again, she heard him tell her, "You need to confess to Almighty God so that I can set you free."

Now that she was near death, he tossed her over his shoulder to bring her topside. It was pitch black outside except for the soft glow of the moon. She wondered what he had planned for her next. He kept talking about asking for forgiveness, cleansing and setting her free. Did that mean he was letting her go?

***

He dropped her unmercifully on the deck of the boat, and as he stared over the sinner an eerie emptiness filled him. Surely he should at least feel empathy for these women, but he had no sense of compassion. It felt as if he was just a shell of a human being, flesh and bones only. He often wondered why God chose him for this mission; there had to be others more worthy than he?

Would he and Mia be together eventually? Would they have children, possibly a son he could show the importance of the mission to?

The need to complete his mission tore at him, and he couldn't hold off any longer. He was ready for Mia to belong to him.

As he tossed her overboard, the body made a loud splash.
She was semi-conscious, barely alive when she hit the
water. The water swallowed her whole, burying her in its
murky depths forever.   Only through death could her soul
be set free. No longer would she tempt men with her body.
No longer would she be able to sin.

Chapter 11

Douglas Thompson opened his eyes and tried to see what time it was. But without his glasses, he was blind. It made no difference as to the time since his bladder was full. He couldn't take any chances at his age by holding it in. Being careful not to wake Amber, he sauntered off to the bathroom.

As he walked into the bathroom, he looked at his watch and saw that it was almost six o'clock in the morning. He would let Amber sleep in while he surprised her with breakfast in bed. The little bakery should be open, and he would go get some beignets and coffee to eat in bed. He hated that this was their last day here. This afternoon it would be back to the real world, where he had to sneak around and see Amber occasionally. Although his heart may not be able to take him seeing her more than he already did. She had an insatiable appetite.

After using the bathroom, he slipped his clothes on, being extra quiet not to wake his sleeping beauty, and headed to the bakery. Once he made it back to the cabin he rummaged through the small kitchen and found a tray to arrange the beignets and coffee on. He had sweet talked the cashier into selling him a few of the flowers they used for decorating the tables. She was more than happy to oblige. You don't find that kind of service up north.

Walking into the bedroom, he whispered, "Honey, I brought you a treat."

Douglas waited for her to reply and when he got no response he moved closer to the bed, "Amber, come on sleepy head I brought you breakfast in bed."

There was still no response. Douglas placed the tray on the corner of the bed and turned on the lamp, surprised to find Amber gone. He walked over to the bathroom to see if she was in there and found it empty as well. He started to panic and called out for her, "Amber! Come on, honey, where are you? I have breakfast."

After he still received no response, he searched the cabin top to bottom. He feared that she had walked out on him. He knew his wallet was still here because he'd used his credit card to buy breakfast. When he called her cell phone, it went straight to voice mail. The rental car was still here, so he knew that she didn't drive off anywhere.

Why wasn't she answering her phone? He wondered where she could be. His gut tightened as panic set in and beads of cold sweat formed on his forehead. He inhaled a quivering breath as he became paralyzed with fear.

He wasn't sure how he should handle this. If he called in and reported her missing, then there was a chance his wife may find out what he had been up to these last few days. Plus his partners wouldn't look too kindly on him having a mistress.

He decided the best thing for him to do was to pack up and leave. Trying to feel less guilty about leaving without her, he convinced himself that she more than likely ran off with a younger man she met somewhere along the way.

Chapter 12

Sundays were Mia's only day off, and she planned on relaxing today. She brewed a pot of coffee. Once it was done, she poured herself a cup and walked outside onto the back porch. She had nowhere to go and wanted to pass the day looking at the bayou, where a light fog hovered this morning. She saw an aluminum skiff pass, most likely going fishing. Another boat was anchored not far from her house fishing. In the reeds along the bank, a heron stood and watched the activity along the bayou.

It was a picture perfect morning. The sky was a vibrant palette of colors above the dense growth of trees on the bank. A mixture of cypress, oak, and weeping willow trees blended in with palmettos and ferns.

Standing here, taking in the scenery, her thoughts drifted towards Detective Chad Picou. Something about him made her want to know more about him. She imagined what it would feel like to be in his tan, muscular arms. She couldn't understand why she thought about him the way she was, being she hadn't formally met the man. She had only seen him from a distance, so there was no way she should be feeling this way about a man she didn't know.

She was being utterly silly. The man probably didn't know she existed.

"Mia?" She jumped at the voice and sent her coffee cup flying. Standing in front of the screen door to her porch was none other than Detective Chad Picou.

"You scared me to death." Mia felt her heart pounding in her chest, but she wasn't sure if it was because he caught her off guard or because she had been thinking about him.

"I'm sorry. I didn't mean to startle you. I saw you walk onto the porch and figured now was probably a good time to come introduce myself. I seem to always miss you."

Mia replied "I've seen you leaving when I am usually coming in."

Chad smiled at her, "I'm sorry I didn't even introduce myself. Detective Chad Picou, your next door neighbor."

Mia took the hand he offered her, "And you already know who I am…"

"I saw you at Mia's the other day and the cashier told me who you were. You seem to have a very popular place."

She laughed, "It appears to be an overnight success. I wonder if it is just because it is new, and the novelty will wear off soon."

"No, it has something to do with the good food and coffee you offer."

"Why thank you. I sure hope you are right."

Mia bent down and picked up her coffee cup that she'd dropped earlier, "Would you care for a cup of coffee. I don't have any beignets, but I can whip us up a breakfast if you are interested."

"I don't want to put you out, but I would love a cup of coffee."

Mia opened the screen door to let him in. As he entered the kitchen, he let out a whistle, "This is one helluva kitchen."

"This is what made me fall in love with the house. I have always dreamed of a house with a gourmet kitchen and when I saw this one I knew I had to have it. The previous owners even installed an outdoor kitchen that is almost just as nice."

She poured them each a cup of coffee, and as she handed him his coffee, she asked, "So how long have you lived here?"

"About two years now. I noticed you moved here not too long ago, what brought you to town?"

Mia responded, "Actually, I grew up here. I moved back from New Orleans and decided to open up a bakery."

It was refreshing to talk to Chad and Mia was glad he stopped by. When Mia looked up, Chad was standing right by her. "I know we just met, but there is just something about you that I find irresistible."

Mia had never believed in love at first sight, but even she couldn't deny that she had feelings for this man. Something about him entranced her.

With him being so close, she couldn't fight the sensations flowing through her. Desire and anticipation swept over her body. He was close enough to kiss. His mouth was alluring, sexy and completely masculine.

Before either could react, Chad had Mia in his arms. He pulled her close and tilted her head up to his. The instant their lips met she knew that she could not deny him. His lips were warm and inviting, making her want to kiss him even more. Mia's arms slid up and wrapped around his neck. She kissed him back with just as much passion as he gave her. His tongue explored her mouth, causing goosebumps to crawl up her body. She let out a soft moan. It had been so long since a man made her feel this way.

***

He found her intoxicating. She tasted so sweet, and he couldn't get enough of her. He needed to stop, but he couldn't bring himself to release her just yet. A turmoil of emotions ran through his body. This woman was unlike anyone he had ever met and kissing her was better than he'd imagined. They had just met, and he couldn't seem to keep his hands off her. She must think he was a total fool.

He finally pulled away and stood there uncertain of what to say.

Mia beat him to it, "I'm sorry. I know this is crazy since we just met, but it's as if I couldn't stop kissing you once we started. I swear I've never done anything remotely like this before."

"You have nothing to apologize for. I made the first move. I don't know what came over me. I've never acted, or felt, like this before."

She smiled up at him, "Maybe we should start off by getting to know each other?"

He was relieved to hear her say that. He was afraid that he had moved too quickly and had scared her off. He looked down at her, "I would like that very much. Would you like to go out to dinner with me one night?"

"How about you come over here for dinner tonight?"

"Dinner sounds good, but I can take you out to eat. It's not necessary that you cook for me."

"I would love to cook for you. Now that I have the bakery I seldom get to cook real meals anymore."

He laughed, "So I take it you are a chef as well as a baker."

"Mais oui. If it hadn't been for the fact that there are already so many restaurants here, I would have opened a restaurant, but there is too much competition. I didn't notice any bakeries here, though, and saw an opportunity."

"That was a wise decision and from the looks of it a successful one."

"Mon Dieu, you have no idea. If I weren't closed on Sundays, I think I would go crazy."

Chad asked, "What time would you like me to come over then?"

"Is seven o'clock too late?"

"I think I can make that work?"

Mia asked, "Do you eat seafood?"

A big grin formed across his face, "I eat anything that doesn't eat me first."

***

After the handsome detective left, Mia couldn't believe what she had done. What had gotten into her? She went from not dating to jumping on the first man who said hi to her.

She rushed off to the bathroom to take a shower and head to the store. It would take her a few hours, but she found a new shrimp recipe she'd been wanting to try, and it sounded like a perfect menu to her. To keep their hands from getting messy, she would peel and devein the shrimp ahead of time. She may even have enough time to bake a loaf of French bread.

By the time Chad knocked on her front door, the house smelled tantalizing from the food she had prepared. She opened the door to let him in, "It smells wonderful. I really didn't expect you to go to this much trouble."

"Come on in. It's no trouble at all. I honestly love to cook."

He handed her a bottle of wine, "I figured since you went through the trouble of cooking I could at least bring a bottle of wine."

She looked up at him, "This will be perfect. Everything is ready."

While they ate their supper, they got to know each other better. Afterwards, Mia couldn't think of anything more romantic than sitting in the moonlight and asked Chad,

"Would you like to take the dessert and coffee to the porch. I love watching the shrimp boats on the bayou at night."

She quickly arranged the white chocolate soufflé and two cups of coffee on a tray. Before heading to the porch, she turned on some music to play in the background. "Make yourself comfortable."

She placed the tray on the coffee table in front of the settee and joined him. Tucking her feet underneath her, she looked out onto the bayou, "If you had asked me two years ago if I would be leaving New Orleans, I would have denied it. I assumed I would be working there forever, never dreaming of owning a business."

Chad asked, "What made you move back home?"

"I walked into my apartment one night while it was being burglarized."

"Did they take anything?"

She answered, "No. The police believe I interrupted the burglar before he had a chance to take anything. The next day I turned in my resignation at the restaurant, canceled the lease on my apartment and made plans to move back home. It turned out since I worked all the time, I had saved up a pretty nice nest egg. So I opened the bakery and found the house. My parents wanted me to move back in with them, but for all our sanity, I knew I needed my own place."

As he leaned in and kissed her, she slid her arms around his neck and kissed him back. His hands moved up her back, sending chills through her body. She wondered what those hands would feel like on her bare skin.

She moved in closer to him, and her body melted into his. She slid her hands under his shirt, needing to make contact with his bare skin. His muscles rippled under her touch.

He whispered in her ear, "Ma douce amie, I know that we just met, but I want to make love to you."

Her senses filled with him and her pulse raced, sending an electrifying tumult charging through her body when she came into contact with his hard, virile body. All she thought about was the sheer ecstasy of being with this incredible man. "I want that too."

By the time they made it to the bedroom, their clothes were on the floor. Mia was more beautiful than he'd imagined. Before Chad made his next move, he looked into Mia's eyes to make sure she wanted to continue. The look in her eyes confirmed more than any words ever could that she wanted him.

The feel of his lips sent delicious shivers of desire down her body. Her blood coursed through her in dizzy anticipation. His lips teased her body, lingering in one spot before moving to a different location.

"You taste so good. I can't get enough of you."

His hands ran over her body, lighting a fire deep inside of her. She heard him groan with need. His touch was a sweet torment. His fingers moved down her body, tantalizing her along the way. He teased her, before he slipped a finger deep inside her. He continued to stroke her nice and slow as he trailed kisses down her body. She felt his tongue enter her and let out a moan of delight. He ran his tongue around the inside of her, teasing every inch of her. He drove her wild with need.

"Oh yes," she let out. There was a need in her voice, a pure wanton and carnal need. Without missing a beat, he brought his finger back inside of her, keeping a steady rhythm while his mouth found her voluptuous breasts one more time. She was wild with need, reveling in the pleasure he was giving her. Desire sent delicious sensations through her body. She cried out in pleasure when the climax hit her.

She couldn't take the sweet torment, "I need you inside of me."

In one swift move, he was inside of her, filling her completely. Her whole body shook uncontrollably. Wave after wave of orgasms rocked her body.

When he woke, he found that Mia was already awake. When he stepped into the kitchen, she was busy cooking breakfast in a clingy, sheer robe.

Mia heard Chad enter the room and turned to greet him. Chad was taken aback at just how gorgeous she was. Mia jumped into his arms and kissed him. He wished he could take her back to the bedroom, but he knew she had to get to work.

She asked, "Are you hungry?"

Smiling, he told her, "Starving. I worked up an appetite somehow."

Mia laughed and poured them a cup of coffee. She prepared him a plate full of food and sat it in front of him. "Wow, I didn't want you to go to this much trouble."

"Trust me, it's no trouble at all and I am more than happy to do it."

Chapter 13

Mia had seen a dress a while back in a boutique near the bakery that would be perfect for the fundraiser. Taking a few minutes after she closed the bakery, and before she had to start on tomorrow's prep work, she rushed over there.

She was thrilled to discover that the dress was still there. As soon as she tried it on and looked at herself in the mirror, she realized that this dress was made for her. The sales clerk found a pair of shoes that matched perfectly with the dress. After checking out, she headed back to the bakery.

Mia's mom would take care of the bakery for her Saturday so that she could be at the hotel in New Orleans early to make sure everything was arranged correctly. Now that everything seemed to be running smoothly at the bakery, she wasn't as worried about leaving someone else in charge for a while. Mia couldn't believe how perfect her life was going. All that she had left was to make sure this fundraiser was a success.

She woke up early Saturday morning. She had to be at the hotel by noon. She gathered her things and left the house. She had a room reserved at the hotel for tonight. She knew that afterwards she wouldn't feel like driving back here, plus she needed a place to get dressed.

When she arrived at the hotel, the hors d'oeuvres were being delivered. She had worked out an arrangement where several of the local restaurants would offer their services free of charge in exchange for special recognition. The restaurants would offer bite size samples of several items available on their menu. So far Mia had kept her out of pocket expenses low, meaning the charity could raise even more money. The tickets for tonight's function cost two hundred fifty dollars per person or four hundred dollars per couple. They would have a band and cash bar available. The bar had promised ten percent of the sales would be donated to the society.

When she entered the banquet room, she noticed the hotel staff was arranging the tables and chairs. Mia started decorating. She placed the tablecloths on the tables and slips to cover the chairs. While she was busy with this, the florist arrived with the centerpieces. "Marie, you outdid yourself this year. They are absolutely incredible."

Looking over the room, she realized it would be breathtaking in here. The hotel staff was busy arranging the silverware and plates now that the tables were ready. At the last minute Mia had collected donations for a small silent auction. She walked over to the auction table to make sure everything was set up there as well. Happy with the way the hotel staff set up the table, she placed the items to be bid on along with a notepad and pen in front of each item. It took longer than she expected to get the silent auction items ready. Guests would arrive in a little over two hours, and the DJ was setting up. She still needed to get dressed so that she was back down here to greet the guests.

Before going back to her room to get dressed, she looked over everything once more. The dance floor and DJ were set up along with the bartender. This had turned out to be one of the biggest fundraisers she had arranged for the local MS Chapter, and she hoped tonight would be a huge success.

After tending to the final details, she rushed up to her room to get ready. As she finished getting dressed, there was a knock at her hotel door. She looked through the peephole and greeted her unexpected guest, "Chad, what a pleasant surprise."

He was speechless when he saw her. She was wearing an exquisite sapphire blue strapless dress that accentuated her sexy body. It clung to her voluptuous curves, leaving nothing to the imagination. "I wanted to surprise you by showing up tonight, but decided I couldn't wait any longer. Shelly mentioned that you had left for New Orleans this morning."

Overjoyed to see him, Mia gave him a big kiss, "This is the best surprise I could ever ask for."

"You look absolutely breathtaking tonight."

Mia smiled up at him, "You look very handsome as well. You clean up nicely."

He waved her off as if he wore a tux every day. She asked, "Do you have a room or are you planning on driving back tonight?"

"I haven't thought that far ahead."

She looked at him shyly, "You are more than welcome to stay with me tonight. I knew I would be too exhausted to drive back."

He gave her a wide grin and reached in the hall for his bag. "I didn't want to impose."

She laughed. "Are you ready to go downstairs? I want to greet everyone as they enter."

After locking her hotel door and handing Chad the key, they rode the elevator downstairs to the lobby. Once in the banquet room, Chad stood near the bar and watched as Mia greeted the guests. She was a natural at this. When he saw a lull in people, he approached her. Whispering in her ear, "Why do you send everyone to the bar first?"

She let out a soft laugh, "To help loosen them up. Plus, the charity receives ten percent of the sales made at the bar tonight."

"You are a shrewd business woman."

"My momma didn't raise a fool."

Chad watched as Mia walked over to the DJ and addressed the group. "I would like to thank everyone for coming tonight. As you know, this fundraiser is for the local Multiple Sclerosis Chapter. They help those suffering from MS, who can not afford their prescriptions, as well as educating the newly diagnosed patients and, of course, help with research to find a cure.

"The silent auction will remain open until nine o'clock. Fifteen minutes beforehand, we ask that all bids be finalized and then the winners will be announced. I would like to thank everyone who donated these wonderful items.

"I would also like to thank the hotel for the use of the banquet room as well as the local restaurants for the excellent food. We truly appreciate it and without your generous donations, tonight would not be possible.

"Please enjoy yourselves. Even though it is a cash bar, ten percent of tonight's total will be donated to the MS Society, so please drink up."

The audience laughed and applauded as she headed to her table. Chad stood up and pulled her chair out, "I'm very impressed with you right now."

"Thank you. This fundraiser means a lot to me. I want to make sure everything is perfect."

Chad responded, "I have been meaning to ask you why you chose this charity."

"My parents weren't able to make it tonight because dad wasn't feeling well. When I was twelve years old he started having a few problems, but swept them under the rug. Well, one morning he woke up and couldn't see. He could no longer keep putting off the ailments that he had been having. Mom took him to the emergency room. And after many subsequent doctor visits and tests, he was diagnosed with multiple sclerosis. He worked for several more years until his legs gave him problems. My dad went from a man who was never sick to someone who had days where he couldn't get around the house. I hated to see how the disease ravaged his body over the years. Dad never complained, but as I got older I became more aware of exactly how much pain he was really in. It broke my heart to know that there was nothing I could do for him. By the time I was sixteen, I was participating in the local Walk for MS and a few other fundraisers. By the time I was twenty-one, I was on the fundraiser committee and have been an active supporter ever since."

"I'm sorry. I didn't realize your family was affected."

She smiled at him, "My Dad is a proud man and doesn't like to tell everyone he has MS. He is afraid they will judge him by the disease and not who he is."

He picked up her hand and kissed it, "Well, if your dad were here he would thank you for doing such a good job. Everything is perfect. You put together a wonderful event." Mia smiled at him and kissed him.

Mia looked around to make sure everyone was having a good time. She noticed several people were sitting at their table and sampling the food. Several other people were on the dance floor dancing and talking.

Chad whispered to her, "Would you care to dance?"

"I would love to." Without another word, they were whirling on the dance floor, his breath hot against her neck. He completely seduced her on the dance floor, and she couldn't wait to get him back up to the room.

The night passed in a haze of passionate dancing and before Mia knew it the DJ was announcing a final call for the silent auction. She was dizzy with desire and tried to compose herself. She headed over to the silent auction tables to retrieve the notepads to announce the winners. She read the winning bids and waited as the winners came to claim their items.

She addressed the crowd once more, "I would like to thank everyone one more time for coming out tonight and for all of your generous donations. This has been our best year yet, and we could not have done any of this without your help."

By the time they made it up to her room, they couldn't keep their hands off one another. Chad kissed her passionately as soon as he closed the door. Her knees grew weak with need as desire exploded through her body. Her whole body shook in anticipation.

Chad whispered in her ear the erotic, wicked things he was going to do to her. Tantalizing things she had never dreamed of. Passionate things that were sure to take her breath away.

As he kissed her, tidal waves of pleasure consumed her body as his lips teased hers. As he swept his tongue inside her mouth, she became lost in a dizzy whirlwind of need.

He carried her off to the bed and yanked off her clothes, not giving her a chance to undress herself, "I need to see you naked."

He quickly stepped out of his clothes. Once he was naked, she took in his body. Muscular athletic legs covered with curly black hair, a washboard abdomen, and a broad chest.

Excitement zinged through her as his gaze devoured her body. He pushed her onto the bed, touching her all over. He trailed a path of hot kisses down her throat, making his way to her breast. He nuzzled her breast and took the tip into his mouth. She moaned in delight as her nipple hardened against his hot tongue. He moved to the next breast, suckling it before gently nipping it with his teeth. She writhed in anticipation. A shiver coursed down her spine, straight to her core at the blatant hunger she saw in his eyes. It was a primitive, carnal lust.

She pulled him close to her and kissed him passionately, "Ah cher, you melt my insides with your kisses."

She blazed a trail of kisses down his body. While she kissed his body, his hands fondled her breasts. His long, strong fingers enveloped them, teasing and plucking at the buds. As she took one of his nipples in her mouth, she could hear his heartbeat racing faster with each kiss.

She brushed her breasts across his stomach as she moved lower down his body. Her body was on fire with need. She was eager to taste all of him before he took her. She took him in her mouth and teased the tip of his erection before gliding him into her mouth. She marveled at the feel of him. She heard him let out a guttural moan.

"It's my turn now cher." He slowly and thoroughly kissed every inch of her. It was as if he was trying to commit her whole body to his memory. As if he wanted to know it as well as he knew his own. She reveled in the feel of him, the masculine scent and taste of him. She let out a needy whimper as her limbs trembled with desire underneath him.

An intense need pulsed through her, primal and basic. "Chad, please I can't take much more," she pleaded with him.

He rolled her over to where she was facing the bed and holding her hips, he thrust deep inside of her. Her body convulsed in pleasure. She closed her eyes and surrendered to the sensations his body brought to hers.

The blend of the physical and emotional feelings was incredible. It was an explosive, provocative combination that brought her to the brink of ecstasy. They found their release at the same time.

Chad sprawled out next to Mia gasping for breath. She turned over and kissed him on the lips. Her warm body curled into him, feeling like silk against his skin. "Ma douce amie. My sweet love, I love holding you close. Si belle, so fine."

Mia woke up gradually, moving one body part at a time. She felt too comfortable to get out of bed. Last night was a dream come true. She breathed in deeply, surrounded by the very scent of Chad. She was completely content. She pressed closer into his hard, muscular body. She fit into him perfectly.

One of his powerful arms was draped across her breasts; the other held her close to him at her hip. This setting was so intimate; too perfect to break the moment by leaving the bed.

None of the other men she had had brief affairs with had ever come close to competing with Chad.

Chapter 14

It was a hot, humid summer day. The threat of rain hung
heavy in the air. A group of laughing girls headed to the
park to play. No one yet had taken much heed to the
warning of the hurricane churning out in the Gulf of Mexico.

Bear Corner, Louisiana was in the far southeast corner of
Louisiana, almost near the Mississippi border. There were
at least four thousand farmers, roughnecks, fishermen and
businessmen that dwelled here. The main livelihood of the
residents was shrimping and working offshore on the oil
rigs. Most of the men here tended to do both. What with
the economy the way it was, shrimp prices were dropping.
So, most shrimpers worked on the rigs and then their two
weeks off were spent crabbing, shrimping, and fishing
depending on the season.

Over the years, this quiet little town had been relatively
lucky when it came to the destruction that could be
associated with a hurricane. Even though the forecasters
broadcast warnings that Bear Corner was directly in the
path, no one was concerned on this Friday night. Even
though there were other bars located near the edge of
town, Cherie's was hopping. As the sun went down,
everyone wanted to drink away their worries and be
troubled with the storm later.   The parking lot was
overflowing with vehicles. Noise poured out of the building.
The sound of laughter mixed with the Cajun band playing
live music.

Cherie's was built on the bayou, inviting boaters and land
lubbers in for the cold beer, good food, and music.

The patrons at Cherie's loved their drinking and loud music on Friday nights. Cherie's catered to a diverse group of people, from roughnecks to fishermen. Occasionally some of the river rats drifted in, but Pierre, the owner, was good at keeping the riffraff out of trouble. He was a burly man who even the toughest of men looking for trouble feared. Cherie's kept the sheriff's office busy on Friday and Saturday nights. By Sunday, the holding cell would be full of belligerent drunks who refused to be escorted home.

Growing up, Detective Chad Picou dreamed of becoming a cop. It seemed like the ideal job when he was a little boy. He would get to run around shooting guns and chasing down the bad guys. He would have a chance to be a true hero.

After graduating from Louisiana State University, he attended the Police Academy and went to work in Baton Rouge. After working there for several years, he came to realize that making rank would be harder than he'd anticipated. There were too many eager officers ready to kiss ass. Picou felt that promotion should be merited on your skills and not how well you brown nosed. When he saw the opening in Bear Corner, he jumped at the opportunity and had never regretted the transfer.

Even though the other residents here didn't seem to be concerned about the impending hurricane, Picou kept a close watch on the forecasts. Right now, it was sitting out there building strength. Some were predicting it would be a Category 3 when it made landfall. This storm could do a lot of damage to this town if caught unprepared.

Chapter 15

The sky was a breathtaking hue of various pinks and oranges. Picou had been told this was what the calm before the storm looked like.

This would be his first up close and personal experience with a hurricane. It would be nothing like living inland when the hurricane made landfall. This time he had to worry about the winds and rain, along with the storm surge. Unlike predicted, Hurricane Henry didn't stay in the Gulf and continue building in strength, but still, it would be a Category 2 when it made landfall in several hours. It would be a nasty storm.

The evening sky lit up like the fourth of July as lightning and thunder made their presence known. The windows in the sheriff's station rattled as the thunder warned of the impending storm. Picou had never experienced anything like this in all of his thirty-four years.

Sheriff Sam Riley walked up to him, "Don't worry, son, this building has held up to worse storms than Henry."

As he talked, Picou watched as the rain poured down from the sky. If it continued to rain like this, the town would be flooded. "The National Weather Service has confirmed that the hurricane is coming to land as a Category 2."

Picou shook his head, "Is that all? At least most of the town listened to the mandatory evacuation, and we don't have too many people to contend with."

Sheriff Riley nodded his head, "This morning, I stopped and checked on a few of the houses where residents had said they were staying, and there are four more families that have left. With the weather forecast stating that we would have at least eighteen inches of rain, they knew we would have city wide flooding. If the storm surge hits us hard, then it will be a long time before the water recedes."

Picou wondered how often the National Weather Service was wrong. "This is a hell of a storm welcoming us into hurricane season."

Sheriff Riley stated, "It has been a good long time since a hurricane has hit this way. I guess it is our turn. I confirmed that the ambulance service and fire department will be on standby. The electric companies have trucks waiting to repair any damage we may suffer. However, they won't work on any downed lines and blown transformers until the wind is below thirty miles per hour. Then, if there is standing water the downed lines still can't be repaired."

The wind picked up. Sheriff Riley informed Picou, "We need to get this last window boarded up before the storm gets worse. We don't need something to fly through a window."

Picou helped Officer Diaz secure the last piece of plywood over the window and they stepped back inside. He still wondered how much protection the plywood would give them when the forces of nature really raged out there. He heard the wind as it whistled through the building. He could picture the trees bending in the wind. He heard objects that had not been secured hitting the plywood sheets.

Sheriff Riley informed everyone, "After the storm has let up we will team up and make our rounds. We need to make sure those that stayed behind don't need rescuing. And if they decided to leave at the last minute, they may be stranded. I look for us to have several feet of water to contend with since we are already below sea level. We will more than likely be using flat bottom boats to get around until the water recedes."

For several hours, they listened to the heavy wind and rain outside. They lost electricity in the middle of the night, but the generator had kicked on three minutes later. So far the generator and building had held up to Mother Nature's recent tirade. As the winds died down, and the National Weather Service had announced that all that remained in their area was the outer bands, they wandered outside to inspect the damage brought on by Henry.

Several feet of water surrounded the town, but as far as Picou could tell no houses were flooded or destroyed. It would be a while before the water receded though. Debris lined the flooded streets, and there were several downed trees. It would take several days to clean up the mess.

Picou noted several stalled vehicles, but so far no rescues. It looked as if everyone made it safely inside and out of harm's way. As he headed to the neighborhoods, the steady purr of the generators filled the air. It would become a familiar sound in the days to come.

Chapter 16

Buddy Grant knew now that the storm had broken this was the best time to go fishing. The storm should have churned up the water something fierce, bringing all the big fish out in search of food. Most of the other town folk left when the mandatory evacuation went into effect. Not Buddy, he had never run scared from a hurricane and he wasn't running from this one. Mais non, this was just a baby storm. Plus, he knew the fishing would be good after Hurricane Henry had struck. He was counting on catching him some nice sized fish. It didn't bother him that the electricity would be out for a while. He had a generator if he needed to use it, but he remembered growing up with no power plenty of times.

As he headed out in his bateau, he noticed the streets were devoid of life. It was strange seeing no cars out at this time of the day. There weren't even people out on their porches. The town was eerily quiet.

They were lucky the water didn't rise any higher, or it would have flooded most of the homes here. He glided the bateau along the streets, being careful to avoid any of the downed power lines. As the water receded, he wouldn't be able to enjoy the use of his bateau as transportation. He noticed several of the older trees were knocked down and lying in the street. The storm was more powerful than he had anticipated, but it still hadn't been too bad for an old timer like himself.

As a breeze blew along the bayou, it brought Buddy back to the memories of his childhood. He grew up in a rickety old house with his parents and siblings, but it had been such happy times growing up. He grew up learning how to live off the land, never spending time inside unless they were forced to by the weather. The kids nowadays don't know what it means to catch your supper. Instead, they spent their time playing video games instead of going outside to play.

This particular area had always been rich in game. It was a sportsman's paradise when it came to fishing and hunting. In today's world his family would be considered dirt poor, but he didn't look at it that way. They always had food on the table and never once went to bed hungry.

He didn't see the body until a slight splash caught his attention. It took a moment for his eyes to focus on the figure half submerged in the dark water. *Mais sa c'est fou*! This was crazy. He knew it was a dead body; it lay there unmoving. Something told him that this wasn't a simple drowning, and he headed back to town quickly.

Chapter 17

A haze settled over the bayou this morning. Summer had returned with a vengeance. It was barely eight o'clock, and it was already ninety degrees outside. Sheriff Riley wiped the back of his neck with a napkin he found in his Chevy Tahoe.

He believed that God had looked over the town and its people when the hurricane made landfall the other day. Now that the water was receding, they could allow residents to check on their property. Those that had generators and wanted to stay would be permitted. The mandatory evacuation that had been issued for the residents had been lifted. All that remained in town were law enforcement personnel in case they had trouble with loitering. Sheriff Riley didn't suspect they would have too much crime to worry with, but you never knew what could happen when a hurricane hit. After the problems associated with other cities when Hurricane Katrina hit, he wanted to be prepared.

The day before landfall, he knew which residents had listened to the mandatory evacuation and which citizens decided to brave it out. In case the waters did start rising, he wanted to know where to send the rescue boats.

He was grateful that Picou had paid such close attention to the weather forecasts and kept him updated. Being from here, Sheriff Riley didn't take too much stock in the warnings issued until that massive storm moved their way. Their saving grace was that it lost strength when it made landfall. But being right at the coast, they still suffered damage.

They had been lucky that the water did not rise high enough to flood many of the buildings, just those houses in low lying areas suffered water damage. It would be another two or three days before electricity was restored, but the power company was working as fast as they could to get it restored.

Beyond the ferns and cypress trees fringing the bayou laid the body. It was partly submerged in the dark, murky water. The smell of death hung heavy in the air. It would be a while before he could rid that smell from his nose. The silence of the morning was broken by the squawk of the radio in his Tahoe.

The dispatcher asked, "Sheriff, Picou wants to know if he needs to head that way."

Sheriff Riley answered her back, "Phyllis, you better send him, the crime scene techs and the coroner. We got a dead body here on Pecan Bayou."

Sheriff Riley went back to the water's edge to observe the body further. *Damn, where did this body wash up from?* The hurricane must have churned up the water something fierce.

Sheriff Riley saw Detective Picou pull up behind his Tahoe. "Do you have any idea who it is Sheriff?"

Adjusting his hat, "No, the body has been in the water too long for easy identification."

It wasn't long before the air was filled with the distant wails of the approaching siren of the ambulance. Dr. Greg Harrison and his assistant got out of the vehicle and joined them.

Dr. Harrison looked over at where the body was, "Do you think it's a possible drowning from the hurricane?" He tried to shield his eyes from the sun while he observed his surroundings.

Sheriff Riley informed him, "No one has been reported missing. I didn't get too close, but it looks as if the body has been submerged for a while. I am hoping to find out more once we fish the body out and move it to another location."

Dr. Harrison looked over at his assistant, "Jeff, go ahead and get your waders on. I need you to get in the water to help with the retrieval. We have to be careful when we move the body. Let's get the body bag underneath it before lifting." Dr. Harrison turned to Sheriff Riley, "It will take all of us to lift the body. We can't just pick it up not knowing how long it has been in the water. We want to avoid as much slippage as possible."

Detective Picou shuddered at the thought. It took some maneuvering to get the body bag under the body. It was much heavier than he would have thought, and the smell became worse once it was moved.

Dr. Harrison looked over at Sheriff Riley, "I believe this is a woman, but the decomposing is so bad that I can't guarantee anything."

The Sheriff confirmed, "No missing reports have come across my desk. Picou, have you heard anything?"

"No, sir. I'll have Detective Melancon call and check the surrounding areas instead of heading this way."

Looking more thoroughly at the body before zipping up the bag, Dr. Harrison informed Sheriff Riley, "This wasn't an accident. Even with the decomposition, it looks as if we may have stab wounds. There are obvious gaps in the skin that are too precise to be made from a propeller or from any form of marine life."

Sheriff Riley couldn't remember the last time they'd had a murder here. He instructed Picou, "While crime scene techs comb the area, I want you to look around and see if you spot anything."

Sheriff Riley had confidence in his crime scene techs, but Picou had eyes like a hawk. He may pick up on something that others may think was insignificant.

It wasn't too much longer when Sheriff Riley heard Picou, "Sheriff you better get over here. I think I got something."

Sheriff Riley trudged his way to the bayou's edge to see what Picou had found. As he neared Picou, he still couldn't make out what the man was looking at, "What have you got?"

"It's a human skull."

Damn, he thought to himself. That must have been one hell of a storm. It must have churned something free from the bottom of the bayou. Sheriff Riley instructed the crime scene techs, "Let's get this entire area roped off. I want this area searched. I want you to turn over every rock. I don't want any area missed. We need to photograph everything, and make sure the location of where you find something is documented." Looking out at the bayou, Sheriff Riley told Detective Picou, "The rest of the body has to be somewhere out there."

"Yes, sir. We need to call and see if the state troopers can send in their dive team."

It took about three hours before the divers were in position and ready. Detective Picou was surprised when they surfaced a few minutes later. He heard the diver shouting something and moved closer to the bayou's edge, "Detective, you have bodies down here; it looks like most were weighed down."

"What do you mean bodies?"

"Meaning you better get several body bags. Offhand, I'd say at least ten, maybe more. We still have a lot of area to cover. It's a graveyard down here. Mostly skeletal remains, but the amount is still staggering."

Holy Crap! Picou never figured anything like this would happen here. They hadn't had any women missing from these parts, so somebody had to be using the bayou for their dumping ground. Who would do this and could they be from here?

Picou heard a rustling behind him and noticed his partner had arrived. "What took you so long, get lost?"

"Bite me. I can't help it that you don't know how to give directions."

***

Detective Jo Melancon knew from an early age she wanted to be a police officer. It was in her blood; her grandfather had been a cop. Her dad may be a shrimper by trade, but he was also a volunteer fireman. Maybe it was something in the Melancon blood that wanted them to be a hero. By the age of ten, she had her life planned out. Although her life may not be going as planned, she did believe she was helping to make a difference here.

After graduating high school, she went to Louisiana State University and completed her four year curriculum with a 4.0 grade point average. She completed her degree in criminal behavior and also studied forensic psychology and profiling methodology.

She came back home and applied to the police force here in Bear Corner. She was the only woman to reach the rank of detective in Homicide. She was the only woman on the police force in this little town. With promotion in rank being limited here in Bear Corner, competition was fierce, and when you added the sexism in, Jo was surprised she had been promoted. But she had aced her test, proving that her knowledge of the law, procedures and investigation process was above par. Following the written exam was the board interview. She sat in front of a bunch of retired and senior detectives where they bombarded her with various questions and scenarios. She aced it, proving to them that she could work well under pressure.

She had been partnered with Detective Picou for less than a year. She had learned over time what his true personality was and that you couldn't change him.

She had worked in a male dominated world for a while now. Most of these men were crude, outspoken and self-absorbed. There were a few men on the force that believed women did not belong there and most of those men had few reservations in exhibiting their chauvinism. Over the years, she had learned how to survive and brush off the comments. Sticks and stones may break my bones, but words would never hurt me had played in her head more than she cared to admit.

She had learned how to survive among these men, laughed at their obscene jokes and indecent proposals and, more importantly, massaged their delicate egos. The one rule she had stuck to over the years was to never get romantically involved with a fellow detective, or police officer for that matter.

Even though she was the only woman, she refused to hide her femininity. She enjoyed dressing like a woman. She even enjoyed the looks she got from men. She would not hide who she was. She had no desire to be one of the boys, but she wanted to be treated as an equal.

She was grateful her partner had never treated her with the same indifference as other fellow officers. As partners, somehow, they could work together without sexism and had even developed a meaningful kinship. Their working relationship had thrived because it was not defined by traditional terms. Mutual respect between the two of them had created a strong foundation on which to build a solid friendship.

"How bad is it?" she asked.

"We have found several skeletons so far and the divers aren't done. It's a watery graveyard down there. The partial skeletal remains are all that remain on some of the cement blocks. I have a feeling this killer has been operating in the area for a while."

"Yeah, but before I came here I did as you asked and searched the missing persons reports. There are not that many in this area. I expanded the search to the New Orleans area, but it is depressing the number of women who go missing there."

"Identification will be a bitch; that is if we can identify them." There was no way they should find this many victims in one area. It just didn't compute. She wondered how long this person had been killing and disposing of the bodies here.

The nude body lying in front of her looked like a balloon ready to burst. All that remained was a shell of a human body, each layer made of water rather than tissue. Her eye sockets were now empty. Her nose, chin, cheeks, and ears had congealed into a featureless mask. They would have to hire someone to attempt to put her facial features back together for a sketch.

If it wouldn't have been for the storm they may have never found out about the watery graveyard. Picou was convinced this was the work of one killer. The question was who could be responsible? Was it someone from here or a fisherman that passed through the area? How long had the mass murderer been dumping bodies in these murky waters? Were there more bodies the further you traveled along the water?

Detective Melancon looked in horror as the skeletons were removed from their watery grave. Until now she thought she had been making this town safe and secure. She was losing confidence in her effectiveness as a cop as the bitter reality set in that a killer lurked in this town, if not on land then on water.

There were so many victims, and they didn't know how they died. The water erased all traces of evidence, and they had no way of knowing if these were women or if they were raped before being killed. She wondered if they were tortured unmercifully before death and she prayed that they were dead before they hit the water.

As she realized the sheer magnitude of this investigation, the mere thought of what these victims must have endured was unimaginable. This would be her first case involving a serial killer. She never fathomed encountering a killer as diabolical as this in her career. How could another human being be so evil?

"Mon dieu, bien mauvais. This was one nasty killer," she exclaimed.

Chapter 18

After Dr. Harrison had made it back to the morgue with the body, she was placed on the autopsy table. He confirmed that she had been dead for over thirty days. Experience had taught him that the tissues soften so much in water they expand far beyond normal dimensions. Water also bleached the skin.

The flesh was completely bloodless, and the slightest touch caused the skin to separate and dissolve. He knew there was no hope of retrieving any evidence off of the body. The bayou made sure of that. Dr. Harrison groaned to himself when he considered his task at hand. His job was going to be difficult. Drowning victims were the worst. Water did strange, horrifying things to flesh.

Working in south Louisiana, this close to the water, he had become an expert on what happened to a body when it had been submerged over time. Unfortunately, there were a few subjects that weren't addressed in depth in medical school and the pathological condition of drowning victims happened to be one of them. Sadly, most of what he had learned had been from experience.

As far as the bones went, they would need to be sent to a forensic anthropologist. Bone analysis was out of his realm of expertise.

But he had an old friend with the FBI who worked with a facial reconstruction artist who was supposed to be an expert. If he agreed to help, he suspected he would want the skeletal remains shipped to their lab instead of coming here where they didn't have the necessary equipment.

He called Dr. Frank Bendell, "Mon ami, it's been a long time, mais non?"

Dr. Bendell replied back, "Mais oui, how are you my old friend?"

"I have been better. I have a case in my morgue right now that may interest your team, but the funds may not be as high as your usual cases."

Dr. Bendell knew that if Dr. Harrison was calling in a favor it must be something big, "What exactly is it that you have?"

"A watery graveyard has been found deep in the bayou here. Several bodies, or I should say skeletal remains, have been uncovered so far. The remains are too far gone for me, and I thought of you and your team. The only way we may be able to identify any of these victims is by facial reconstruction, and I know your assistant is one of the best in her field."

"That she is. How many are we talking about?"

"Last count they pulled fifteen bodies out of the water, but there could be more. They are sending in a special robot to travel along the bayou floor, but some may have sunk too deep to make recovery possible."

"Mon Dieu, you have a mass murderer on your hands, mais non?"

Dr. Harrison replied, "Mais oui."

Dr. Bendell instructed him, "Box up what you have and send them as soon as possible. My team and I will not charge you as long as we are allowed to write a journal about this case."

"I will run it by Sheriff Riley, but I don't see where he would have a problem with that. Everyone wants to put these poor souls to rest, mon ami."

"Good, good. Just let me know when you have an answer and if you send me the remains. We will get to work on them as soon as possible."

Chapter 19

He woke up this morning with unsettled emotions. He had
yet to finish God's mission, and he wasn't sure how much
longer he could wait for his sweet Mia. The world had too
many sinners that needed saving, and it was a daunting task
to complete. He worried that this was a charge he would
never finish.

His body yearned for Mia. How much longer must he wait
to make her his? He prayed God would answer him soon.
He knew better than to doubt God's plan. He should
consider himself special, God chose him to be His divine
messenger. He would wait until God told him he could make
her his. Continuing God's mission was the only thing that
mattered right now.

After saying his morning prayers, he brewed a pot of coffee
and walked outside to get his daily paper. When he saw the
front page story, he knew God had just spoken to him.
Soon Mia would be his.

Sitting at the kitchen table with his cup of coffee and paper,
he read the article in more depth. The top story was not
about the hurricane, but about the mission God had him on.
His heart swelled with pride. Today everyone would be
talking about his work.

The reporter stated that skeletal remains were recovered
from the bayou, having been stirred up by the hurricane
that ravaged this area. Hurricane Henry must have been
God's way of releasing the bodies from their watery grave.

Now he knew it was God's will for him to purify this town of sinners for Mia.

The article did not give too much information other than bodies having been found. He wondered if the local sheriff's department would be handling the case or if they would have to bring in outside help, maybe even the FBI.

If there were enough of a public outcry, they would have no choice but to bring in outside help. He must be careful now that they knew about his work; he could not be caught.

Chapter 20

The discovery of the bodies had this town in shock. Mayor
Russ Daigle had been riding Sheriff Riley's back daily. He
stressed that he expected some leads in this case and
quickly. The local paper had been trashing the police
department, calling the department inept and wondering
when the FBI would be brought in.

Picou had a difficult time getting everyone to understand
that it would be a long and arduous investigation. He
couldn't just pull a suspect out of thin air. He had a job to
do, and he would do it, but he wanted it done right. He had
no control over the press. Besides, he was a detective and
not a damned public relations officer. Let someone else
worry about handling the press.

At least everyone was in agreement to permit Dr. Harrison
to send the remains off to be examined by a forensic
anthropologist and his team. It may be their only hope to
identify these poor victims.

This case had folks spooked. They saw a potential killer
lurking about in every shadow. They wanted someone
arrested quickly for this heinous crime.

He worried every morning that this would be the day they
were called into Sheriff Riley's office and informed the FBI
had been called in. Each day that they failed to produce a
viable suspect escalated the chance of this happening.

There would be no warning when it happened. No amount
of begging would help once the decision was made.

Unlike other cases Detective Picou had worked on in the past, this one had him baffled. His acute investigative skills and inherent ability to unearth a clue from out of nowhere was something he was known for. This time they were dealing with a crafty killer.

Needing a break from the investigation, he called Mia, "Are you in the mood for an evening of sumptuous food, stimulating conversation and dessert in bed?"

Mia could think of nothing better, "I am on my way home. I will cook us supper so that we don't have to go out."

"Are you ever going to let me take you out to a restaurant?"

She laughed, "Maybe one of these days, but after spending all day in one I would rather stay at home."

As Chad hung up with Mia, he felt his heart stretch and swell a little at the thought of Mia cooking supper for him.

***

Mia had just finished cooking supper when the doorbell rang. She opened the door to let him in, "I have been thinking about you all day."

He kissed her thoroughly, "I couldn't get over here fast enough to see you. I need to forget about today for a little while."

She loved Chad's kisses. She loved the way his lips moved sensually over her mouth, his tongue teasing her lips until seeking entry. Just a simple kiss from Chad could arouse her to the point of dizziness.

When Mia realized she was in love with this man it sent euphoria rushing through her. She had always dreamed of falling in love with a man like Chad Picou, dreamed of having a marriage like her parents. She wanted someone warm and loving, supportive and giving. She needed someone who she could tell her innermost secrets to without fear of being judged. Someone she could come home to after an emotionally draining day and know he would make her feel better. Someone she could have a family with, give her heart to and not someone who she was just physically attracted to.

Walking into the kitchen, "Supper smells great."

Mia walked up to him, pressing her body into his and kissed him one more time. She couldn't get enough of him.

When his lush mouth made contact with hers, she forgot about the food she had cooked. She could not fight the tidal wave of desire that washed over her.

She let him kiss her, moaning his name. She gave in to the exquisite, sensation of being wanted above anything else.

She wanted him and he wanted her. She wanted to lose herself in desire. Just the smell of him was intoxicating. Her pulse raced as she wrapped her arms around his neck.

His lips were hot and moist against hers. Her breath came in deep gasps. She had an expression of profound enjoyment on her face. Her touch was soft and delicate, sliding over his body like silk. His touch sent pure need to her very core.

She let her hands wander over his body. Her fingers massaged every cord and muscle of his arms, lingering on the contours of his rock hard biceps.

As he caressed her body, she didn't think she had ever been touched so lovingly, so tenderly. She had never felt anything so torturous yet glorious at the same time. His hands on her felt so good, so right. He kissed her once more, placing a hand on the middle of her back and pulled her closer to him, into his aching need. He suckled her wonderful lips, tangling her tongue with his.

As her fingers worked their way to his groin, he thrust his tongue even deeper into her mouth. She moaned against his lips.

She undressed him right there in the kitchen, supper forgotten. She explored his body with her velvet lips. Her tongue created havoc on his body. Everywhere his hands touched brought her scorching pleasure. She wanted him so badly at this moment. She couldn't imagine herself ever not wanting him.

He picked her up and carried her off to the bedroom. He kept kissing her madly, tossing her onto the bed and tumbling on top of her. Her body arched up into his, grinding deliciously into him.

"Ah cher," he whispered into her ear.

***

This woman was incredibly provocative. Her slumberous, sexy eyes made him weak in the knees. Desire for her permeated every inch of him. He looked down at her luscious nude body, devouring her with his eyes.

He flipped her over where she was now on top of him. Her voluptuous breasts hung full and ripe above him, begging to be suckled.   Her long legs straddled him. His pulse raced at the sight of her naked body straddling his. She rubbed against him, slow and tantalizing. He thought he would explode with that one simple movement. He needed her to slow down; they had all night.

Mia reached over him and removed a feather from her nightstand. "I thought you would need to relax a little tonight, so I planned a treat for you."

He looked at the long, supple feather, "What do you have planned, cher?"

She smiled enticingly, "Lie back and enjoy Detective." She slowly drew the feather across his jaw line, letting it glide along his body.

She held the feather just above his taut nipple teasingly, "Do you want me to stop?"

"Mais non." She lowered the feather tickling his nipple ever so lightly. He hissed out a gasp from the torturous pleasure. As she moved to his other nipple a zing of arousal singed through him.

She heard him let out another moan, "Do you like that?" she asked him.

"Mais oui."

She continued teasing him with the feather further down his body, creating a delicious torment of desire. His whole body shuddered with excitement. "Ah Cher." A cascade of goose bumps followed in the wake of the quill. Slowly she let the feather glide along his erection. It was sheer torture for him.

She took him in her mouth. He was long, thick and scalding hot. Suddenly she was on her back with him straddling her. "Je suis en feu," he informed her, "I'm on fire for you."

His hands wandered over her body, savoring the feel of her hot skin. It was utterly enchanting to have his hands on her body. He cupped one of her breasts and caressed her nipple. He took the hard point into his mouth. Mon Dieu, she felt so good. He didn't know if he could restrain himself tonight.

She moaned in pleasure. Her eyes were heavy with desire. He wanted to ravish her until they were both sated. He couldn't take this sweet torture anymore. He lowered his body to hers, fitting perfectly into her pliant curves. He had needed this, to feel her naked body underneath his. "I love how you taste, so intoxicating."

"And I love the way you make me feel," she replied back in quick gasps.

Her hips were doing a slow undulation against him as her feet moved up his legs. He let out a moan as he thrust inside of her, filling her with him. With each thrust he moved in deeper, further and further until he swore he was touching her very core. His eyes never broke contact from her, dazzling in the pleasure coursing through her. She writhed underneath him, seeking more and more of him.

Their bodies pulsed to the same beat. They were melded together. Never before had he ever felt so drunk with desire. Her muscles tightened around him, pulsing against him. He thrust deeper into her.

She cried out in sweet release. A thousand searing sensations rippled through his body. With a deep groan, he erupted deep inside of her. He held her tight while she rode the storm.

Chapter 21

Today had been the worst day Jo Melancon had had since joining the force. She called it a night and headed home. All she wanted was to grab a bite to eat, curl up in bed and fall fast asleep.

Not in the mood to stop at a restaurant and risk running into anyone that wanted to talk about the case, she decided to bake a frozen pizza in the oven.

Once at home, she went into the kitchen, opened her fridge and grabbed a beer. She reached into the freezer and grabbed the first one readily available and put it in the oven. While waiting for the pizza to cook, she turned on the TV. Not much was on but at least its mindless babble would prevent her mind from over thinking the case.

As soon as the timer went off she pulled the pizza out of the oven and sliced it. It's sad that lately takeout and frozen food had become a staple in her house. She really should learn how to cook, but she didn't like to cook for one person. It was easier to grab something to eat on the way to wherever she was going or pop something in the microwave.

Now and then her mom cooked her several dishes for the freezer. Although, lately, her mother had nagged her to learn how to cook, and find herself a man. Jo suspected that learning to cook may be easier than finding a man.

Her mother even bought her several cookbooks hoping to inspire her to cook a dish. One of these days she would attempt to cook again.

Just the other night Jo felt adventurous and tried to cook a shrimp stew. She went to the local grocery store and purchased the ingredients she thought she needed. In hindsight, she should have read a recipe. Jo doubted even a dog would have eaten that concoction. She had no idea what she did wrong, but it didn't even resemble shrimp stew. That unfortunate disaster had curtailed any future attempts to cook.

After finishing supper and finding nothing on TV, Jo decided to curl up in her bed. She tossed and turned for the three hours as sleep eluded her. With a pounding headache, she gave up on slumber and reached for her ibuprofen. This particular brand had an added benefit of a sleeping aid. When her headaches were this bad it seemed to be the only thing that helped her.

Her mind was racing through the events that had taken place here in the last few days. None of this made any sense. There were so many missing persons' reports to review, and so little hope in identifying the victims.

A facial reconstruction specialist was working with them to identify some of these poor souls. It would still be a long and laborious process.

She wasn't sure why this case was affecting her this way. She had always prided herself on being able to separate her emotions from her job. Several cuts and breaks were discovered on the bones confirming that these victims were tortured before dying.   The one victim that Dr. Harrison could autopsy had water in her lungs, which meant that she was alive when the killer threw her into the bayou.

When she closed her eyes she could feel their fear and hear their screams, their pleas begging for mercy. This man had no pity or human compassion.

As her medicine kicked in, she hoped that when she closed her eyes she would dream without seeing the bones of the victims, without hearing their pleas for help.

Chapter 22

He watched as she exited the bar and walked into the humid night air. The cloudless sky was set ablaze with twinkling stars. He tried to say she had changed her life around, but yet this sinner still worked in Satan's den. Alcohol was one of Satan's most insidious servants. Drunken heathens tarnished their souls through the sins of the flesh in Cherie's and the other bars.

The moonlight helped illuminate his way. He took a deep breath and let the bayou air fill his lungs. A smile creased across his face, and his heart pounded.

It was time for her to be absolved of her sins. It was time she confessed her worldly sins. Oh yes, he knew she had sinned. She was ready to ask for forgiveness, to give her life for the one he loved.

***

Night had fallen, and the security lights were on in the bar's parking lot. The darkness cloaked the bayou in varying shades of black. The noise of the bar faded, competing out here with a chorus of frogs singing and the incessant chirps of crickets. The air was fresh with the scents of the season. She breathed in the smell of the jasmine, wisteria, and honeysuckle as it mixed with the dank smell of the bayou.

Misty Olivier had worked at Cherie's for going on two years now. If they didn't need the extra money, then she would be at home with her family. But money was tight and every extra little bit helped. Ever since the moratorium on offshore drilling was put into effect, her husband's pay had been cut. She kept hoping that the freeze would be lifted, but it had been a slow process. Tonight she was dead on her feet, but at least it was a short walk home.

The skin on the back of her neck prickled with fear when a noise from behind startled her. She slammed a hand to her heart as terror took over her senses. A figure appeared from the shadows, simply staring at her and saying nothing. His eyes glittered in the eerie silvery light cast from the moon. A shiver of apprehension snaked down her back. She started to second guess her decision to walk home, maybe she should have asked Jeff, her husband, to come and pick her up tonight.

She wasn't sure what was happening. At first she didn't notice, but as the fog lifted from her mind she realized she was restrained to a table. Her head felt heavy, her hands clumsy. Her body didn't want to cooperate. She knew this man, grew up with him.

"So now you know," he whispered in her ear. His voice chilled her to the core. She cringed in fear. "Today is the most important day of your life. You must pay for your sins. Are you ready for your soul to be cleansed?"

His cold eyes staring down at her could only mean her time had come. This was not how she wanted to die. She felt his eyes glaring at her breasts, as goosebumps covered her body. She couldn't help but shiver.

The smell of incense burning filled the room and he incessantly chanted a prayer. Sheer terror curdled her blood as her throat constricted. She tried to free herself, but the restraints were too tight. Was he the man who had dumped the bodies in the bayou? Could he really be that cruel?

Although she was terrified to death, her feisty nature took over. A charge of bitter reality surged through her; unbridled rage pulsed through her body. She had always been told she was too strong willed, sometimes to a point beyond reason. The thought of him touching her made her cringe. "What's wrong, you can't get a woman any other way than by abducting her and tying her up? I bet you can't even get it up."

When she saw the rage in his eyes, she realized that maybe she had pushed him too far. She should keep her mouth shut just this once, especially if she wanted to live through this.

"I don't want your body, I want to save your soul," he seethed to her.

She let out a crazed laugh. "What gives you the right to judge me?"

"You are a sinner and must be cleansed." She looked into his eyes and saw a craziness there that scared her. Maybe if she agreed with him, he would let her go.

He walked towards the table, calm and in control. She flinched at the sight of the knife. It cut through her flesh, sending white hot pain searing through her body. *Why is this happening to me?* The room spun as the pain assaulted her body. Terror clawed through her brain. She desperately tried to free herself. She watched in horror as her blood pooled on the floor.

She pleaded with him, "Please, please spare me. I have sinned, I beg for your forgiveness." He smiled, glad that she had confessed to her sins.

"Please, you don't have to hurt me anymore. I confess to Almighty God that I have sinned." She felt her strength failing. She had no energy left to fight. The image of her captor's face blurred. She became weak; her attempts at survival were frail and futile. Her body went limp.

"You must atone for your sins," he informed her. "It is God's word."

When she regained consciousness, she felt as if she had been run over by a semi truck. Her face throbbed in pain, along with the rest of her body.

This demented man was unrelenting in his dark, deadly purpose. She was ready for death; the pain had become unbearable. His brutal strength was no match for her. Agony tore through her at the realization she would never see her husband and child again. When she looked into his eyes, she could see the true depths of his evil.

The deluge of her past sins, of those she had wronged washed over her. There were so many people, some who had loved her and she hurt them. She tried to make up for it, sought to make a better life, but it was too little, too late, and this was her punishment. Would her son remember her? Would her husband mourn her death or would he let her death turn him bitter? Would he marry again? Would her son call the new wife mommy? Would anyone know what happened to her?

* * *

Her death did not come mercifully. Her screams became almost deafening. Pain was an integral part of redemption. It excited him immensely when he cleansed a tormented soul.

With a glow of victory in his eyes, he grinned as he looked over her lifeless body, "In the name of the Father, the Son and the Holy Spirit I release you my child. Your soul is cleansed. Go in peace."

Now that he had been found out it wouldn't be as easy to dispose of the bodies by sinking them to the bottom of the bayou. They were looking for him so he must change how and where he disposed of the bodies. The closer he moved to the Gulf of Mexico the riskier it would be to get rid of her. The most effective manner for ensuring the adequate obliteration of her body was to dispose of it from the bow of the boat while underway. The body would travel under the hull of the vessel and thru the propellers.

Making sure no one was near, he tossed her overboard and prayed God forgave her sins and let her into His Kingdom.

Chapter 23

The call came in not long after midnight. Unfortunately, criminals didn't look at their watches before committing a crime. If police officers were paid for every hour they spent performing police-related duties they could retire by their fortieth birthday. There was no such thing as a daytime shift. You never knew what hours you would work, especially during an active investigation.

He groaned as he answered his cell phone. Detective Picou knew that odd hours and late nights were part of his job.

He tried to keep his voice down, not wanting to wake Mia. After he had hung up with the dispatcher, Mia looked over at him and asked, "What's wrong,"

He leaned down and kissed her, "Missing woman."

Mia pushed herself upright and propped her back against the pillows. "That doesn't sound very promising."

"According to dispatch a distraught husband called in when his wife didn't return home tonight after work. I'll be back as soon as I can."

As he stepped outside, the mugginess of the night hit him. The smell of the bayou hung heavy in the air. The streets were devoid of life as he headed to Misty Olivier's house. He had a bad feeling about this. He prayed that their killer hadn't started hunting the women of Bear Corner.

He called Melancon, "I didn't wake you, did I?"

"Nah, I'm out running right now. So, since you are seeing Mia I guess this isn't a booty call." She and Picou had a relationship where they could joke back and forth and neither took it to heart. She also hoped to add a little humor to what would be a rather grim night.

"Just got a call about a local woman reported missing."

Melancon felt the dread building up inside of her, "Crap. Who filed the report?"

"Her husband called it in. Claims she should have been home from work hours ago. He went looking for her and couldn't find her. Cherie's said that she left work at her usual time."

"What time did she get off?"

"She got off at eleven and walked home."

Jo pulled herself out of bed and got dressed. "Where are we meeting?"

"Everyone is meeting at her house. Her husband would rather not wake up their son again, and he didn't want to call her mother and worry her needlessly right now."

Melancon let out a sigh, "I'll meet you over there, what's the address?"

Melancon pulled up at the same time as Picou. She asked, "Do you want to take the lead on the interview?"

"That's fine; I can do that."

The Olivier house was a typical shotgun house found in this small neighborhood. In larger towns, these would be considered starter homes, but here this was where you raised your families. Most were small two bedroom homes. Only a few in this neighborhood had three bedrooms. The Olivier's lived in one of the smaller two bedroom homes.

It didn't take long for Mr. Olivier to answer the door. He was dressed in a pair of cargo shorts, T-shirt and flip flops, typical Louisiana attire. His brown hair was cut short and looked unkempt.

Picou offered his hand. "I'm Detective Chad Picou and this is my partner, Detective Jo Melancon."

After shaking hands, Mr. Olivier opened the door for them to enter the house. They made their way over the toys cluttering the floor, and Picou sat in the recliner while Melancon took the couch. Mr. Olivier paced the floor instead of sitting, clearly distraught.

He looked at them with fear in his eyes, "Do you think she is dead?"

Melancon hadn't expected him to ask that question right away. Picou informed him, "Right now there is no evidence to support that possibility."

"But what about the bodies found in the bayou? You can't tell me that this is a coincidence. I don't like that as soon as the bodies were found my wife disappears."

Picou tried to calm him down, "Mr. Olivier there is nothing to confirm that the man who killed those people lives here. Besides, nothing has led us to believe that any of the victims are from here. We have had no missing persons' reports filed."

He looked at Picou, "Until now. I am so afraid that you will come knocking on my door to tell me you found her at the bottom of the bayou."

"When did you last hear from your wife?"

"She picked me up from work at five o'clock. I dropped her off at work afterward and came home."

"I take it she walks home from work?"

"Sometimes she calls to ask that I come get her, but she doesn't like to wake up our son. It saves us on gas if I drop her off at work instead of going back and forth too many times."

Jo Melancon cringed at the thought of what this poor woman may be going through. She sure hoped that their killer didn't have her.

Picou hated this part of the interrogation, "I have some questions I need to ask you. Please don't take offense to these next few questions. How long have you been married?"

"Almost seven years."

Picou continued, "Everything okay with your marriage?"

"We had our moments over the years, but nothing out of the ordinary. Money has been tight, which is why she works at Cherie's. She had a hard time finding a job that allowed her to work either nights or days when our son is in school. Jacques over at Cherie's offered her the hours she needed, so she jumped on it."

After leaving the Olivier residence, the police detectives elected to drive over to the police station. Once they made it back to the precinct, Picou asked his partner, "So, what do you think?"

"It is too big of a coincidence that as soon as the bodies are discovered a local girl goes missing."

"I feel the same way. We need to find this killer before Mr. Olivier becomes a widower."

Picou looked over at Melancon, "I want to nail this guy. His ass needs to fry."

Chapter 24

Paul Adams adjusted the air conditioner in his car as the sun continued to beat down on him. He never thought he would travel outside of New Orleans for a news story, but when his boss caught wind of this one he didn't want to just reprint the article from the local paper. Oh no, he had to send a reporter to Bear Corner where the story actually was.

Pulling over at the first place he came to, Pop's One Stop, he grabbed something to drink and possibly ask a few questions. He learned a long time ago to talk to the locals first because they knew the town gossip. Looking around the little gas station, it had seen its better days, but it was still very busy.

Before exiting the car, he grabbed his tablet in case he needed to take some notes. Once outside of his car, the oppressive summer heat hit him. The high humidity had him feeling like he was standing inside a sauna. He had no doubt it was well over one hundred degrees today.

He ran his hands through his thick hair, making sure nothing was out of place and felt the perspiration already forming. Paul despised this weather. He was ready for the cooler days of fall.

This would be one of those days he thanked his dad for his Cajun accent. He had started to lose it when he went to college up north, but after moving back down here, it seemed to be returning. He got his looks from his mother, so until he talked most of the locals took him for a northerner. Of course, this far south most of the Cajuns here considered a northerner anyone north of I-10. He had to agree that it was a different culture here.

Paul was proud of his good looks. He stood over six feet tall, had a full head of dark blond hair and a pair of baby blues to go with the whole package. Girls tended to fall all over him when he entered a room.

He stepped into the small store and headed to the cooler for a soft drink. The burly man behind the register watched Paul, trying to place him. "You not from 'round here?"

After getting his soft drink, he headed to the register, "No, sir. I came to do a story on the bodies found out in the bayou."

"Ooo Eee! Dat's a sad t'ing dat's for sure. Now who would want to go and do a t'ing like dat to someone? What dis world coming to?"

Paul realized he may get more information from him than he had originally suspected. "It's a shame that's for sure. Do they have any suspects?"

"Mais non, but it couldn't be anybody from here. Whoever did dat must be filled with hate; dat's not someone from here."

Paul asked the local, "Did they identify who the victims were?"

He shook his head, "Mais non, they don't t'ink it's any from here. No one is missing. You should stick around. We having a fais do do tonight. Try to lift everyone's spirits."

Paul had no desire to spend the night down here, but if it gave him the chance to talk to more locals, or at least listen to the gossip around town, it would be worth the misery.

"Is there a place to stay around here?"

"Mais oui, right down da road is Cajun Cabins."

It didn't sound too promising, but if it helped him land a story, it would be worth it. "Thanks so much. Guess I'll see you tonight then."

As soon as Paul pulled up to Cajun Cabins he was impressed, it wasn't what he expected. They were actual houses. He hoped his boss didn't have a fit when he saw his expense report. Stepping into the office his breath was taken away by the woman behind the counter. "The man from Pop's One Stop told me about you. He said you may have a room for tonight."

She looked him over, "We have one camp left. Usually, dad wants me to get more than a night's stay, but I guess since he sent you, he will let you rent for one night."

He looked at her in surprise, "That man is your dad and he owns both places?"

"Yeah, he's got a pretty good racket going if you ask me. He bought these places when the owners wanted to move away after the hurricane. Bought them for next to nothing. Now when people stop at the station for a place to stay if he likes them, he sends them this way."

Paul let out a laugh, "Yeah, I guess he has the perfect business plan. How much will a night's stay cost me in one of his cabins?"

"It's two hundred twenty-five dollars a night or one thousand for the week."

Paul's boss would have some choice words, but he handed her the company credit card just the same. "One night for now. I work for a paper in New Orleans and came to cover a story on the bodies that were found."

"Yeah, that's a shame. No telling how long they have been down there. If it hadn't been for that hurricane, they might have never come to the surface.

That night, Paul followed the music to find the fais do do. All around him were people looking forward to having a good time. He heard several people laughing, talking and telling ribald jokes in Cajun French.

This trip may have been worth it, after all. He even talked to the fishermen who found the body.

As soon as he made it back to his cabin, he began writing his article,

> Several days ago a fisherman in the town of Bear Corner discovered the body of an unidentified young woman. Although authorities have yet to release a formal statement, reliable sources on the scene confirmed that the death was a homicide. A number of other remains were also discovered, leading authorities to believe

this killer has been lurking in the shadows
for some months, if not years……..

Now he needed to find something to follow up on. The next morning he got the break he had been waiting for, a local woman had gone missing.

Chapter 25

Mia spotted the reporters camped out in downtown Bear Corner as soon as she arrived. It didn't take long for word to spread. They were standing around, clustered in small groups, reminding her of those waiting for the parades during Mardi Gras in New Orleans. Being wary of the reporters, she rushed toward the bakery, hoping to avoid the vultures.

When Mia saw a man standing near the bakery, she prayed he was just waiting for her to open. Dread filled her as he walked towards her. Paul Adams called out, "Miss, can I talk to you a minute, please?"

Shaking her head as she tried to ignore the man, Mia briskly walked to the front door, "Miss, please. I won't take up much of your time. I just want to ask you a couple of questions."

Mai shook her head in disapproval and told him, "I don't have anything to say."

She was almost at the door when he stepped in front of her, "Please I just want to ask you a few questions about the possible missing woman."

"You probably know more than me," she answered, which was most likely true. She had waited for Chad to return to her house last night, but he called to say he would be tied up most of the night and that she should go back to bed. She tossed and turned last night thinking about what the poor woman's family must be going through.

"I can get your name in the paper and give you some free advertising for your new bakery." He persisted.

"I have nothing to say." Once inside the bakery, she locked the door. Hopefully, by the time she opened, he would have given up on wanting to talk to her.

A buzz of activity filled Mia's this morning. The reporters loitering around downtown found their way in here. But at least the reporter from this morning had left her alone. People were waiting, elbow to elbow, to place their orders. The smell of freshly brewed coffee filled the air. Mia had a hard time keeping the display cases filled with goodies.

After two hours had passed, customers were still pouring into the bakery. From lifting all the dough and standing hours on end cooking, her back was vehemently protesting. Business had been fantastic today, she was almost sold out and she still had two more hours before closing.

When the customers dwindled down, she finally had a few moments to get caught up on a few things. As she opened her mail, Mia's blood ran cold. She read the letter a second time, trying to make sense of it.

> Soon my love we shall meet. My mission is almost done. There are only a few left that must be saved. What I have done, I have done for you.

Along with the note was a necklace with a small diamond pendant. A chill ran through her body as she read the note. Without hesitation, she called Chad. She needed to tell him about this note, especially with the bodies that had shown up recently and now a missing woman.

He answered on the first ring, "Picou."

"Chad, it's Mia. I know you are busy, but I just received a note in the mail and I think you may want to see it. I'm not sure if it has something to do with what you are investigating or not."

Chad's curiosity was piqued, "What kind of note did you get?"

"I got a note from a secret admirer informing me that he only has a few more souls to be saved. There's something else. When I was living in New Orleans I would get these little trinkets in the mail. I always thought they were from fans of mine at the restaurant. The owner was big into making his chef's presence known so it never bothered me. Which was why I thought nothing of the trinkets when I started getting them here."

Chad asked her, although he wasn't sure if he wanted to know the answer, "Just how many trinkets are we talking about?"

"I'd have to count for sure, but at least fifteen, maybe more."

Chad thought back to the number of bodies he had to identify and, unfortunately, that figure fit. "I don't suppose you still have the trinkets do you?"

"The ones that I received here are at the bakery in my desk, and the ones from New Orleans are at the house."

Chad asked, "Are you at the bakery right now?"

"Yeah, I'm working later than normal today. We had a few orders come in right before closing."

He informed her, "I'm on my way over right now. I am bringing a forensics tech with me so he can take your fingerprints to compare with those found on the note and other packages."

"That's fine. I'll be here."

***

As Picou headed to Mia's bakery, he wondered what her connection was to the killer if it was indeed the killer contacting her. He didn't like this one bit.

By the time Mia made it home, she was restless and couldn't quiet her mind. Chad mentioned earlier that he wouldn't see her tonight with the recent missing person case looming over his head.

After trying to watch a movie with no success, she changed into a pair of shorts and tank top. Maybe a good walk would tire her out enough to where she could sleep.

She took a few minutes to do her warm up stretches, and then headed out down the road. No matter how hard she tried to clear her head with each step she kept going over today's events. Nagging thoughts of the little gifts she had received over the years plagued her.

Hopefully, Chad found other fingerprints on the items besides hers. She was worried that he wouldn't find any, meaning that whoever sent them knew to be extremely careful.

Half a block from her house, a sudden uneasiness came over her. At first she tried to ignore the feeling. She was walking on a perfectly safe street, and nothing ever happened around here. Then she remembered Chad was helping search for a missing woman who had been walking home from work last night.

She couldn't shake this uneasy feeling, and with each step, the feeling grew worse. Someone was watching her. Without breaking stride and trying not to be too obvious, she looked around, her gaze taking in both sides of the

street. So far she didn't see anything out of the ordinary.
She saw nothing sinister or threatening lurking about. She
was just being silly, her mind working overtime from all the
events that had occurred in the last twenty-four hours.

Even at this hour the air was thick with humidity. As she
headed back home, she was dripping with sweat. She had
been told sweat was good for you, that it helped detoxify
your body. If that was the case, then she should be healthy
as a horse with the amount she had sweated. Mia doubted
whoever came up with that theory lived in South Louisiana.

Her walk did nothing to relax her. Her nerves were more
strained than before. Maybe a long shower would help.
Walking into the bathroom, she turned on the shower and
undressed. Once in the shower, she let the hot water pulse
against her back.

After toweling off, she blow dried her hair, smoothed her
favorite scented body lotion all over and slipped into a pair
of boxer shorts and tank top. She had a book that she
wanted to read and maybe it would help get her mind off
her other problems.

Before settling in with her book, she put on a load of
clothes. She went to the kitchen and poured a glass of
Moscato sparkling wine and prepared a plate with some
Brie and crackers to snack on. She should be tired of sweets
after a day like today, but she had been waiting to try this
wine all day.

She curled up on the couch with her treats and opened the
book. After she had started reading it, she realized it wasn't

a book she should have chosen for tonight. It was about a serial killer stalking a small southern Louisiana town.

Soon, her eyelids drooped, and she fell sound asleep. She dreamed about Chad. He was in her blood, like a drug. When he was away from her, like tonight, she couldn't wait to see him. Could this be love? Could he be the one?

He stirred a hunger in her that she didn't know was possible. As she drifted deeper into sleep, her doorbell rang. Having just dozed off, she was still disoriented. She looked through the peephole and her spirits lifted. "I thought you were working tonight."

Chad kissed her as he moved inside, "Jo and I were getting tired and realized we wouldn't do anyone any good if we didn't get some sleep. I noticed your lamp on and decided to see if you were still awake."

Mia was so glad to see him. She reached up and wrapped her arms around his neck and kissed him. She heard him sigh as he kicked the door closed. Never letting her go, he locked the door and carried her off to the bedroom.

While in his arms, she let her mouth trail kisses down his neck. She could tell she was affecting him already. She would never tire of being in his arms. His chest was strong and hard, with little hair.

Desire sent butterfly flutters in her stomach as he set her on the bed. She slowly took off his shirt, letting her mouth trail kisses along his upper torso. Her tongue traced circles around his already hard nipples. She was wet with excitement.

She felt his erection pulse through his pants. She unbuttoned his slacks, and eased them off of him. She moved lower down his body and let her lips brush up hard against him. She heard him moan as he wrapped his hands in her hair. The sounds he made were erotic and a turn on.

He pulled her back up and undressed her slowly. "It's your turn now," he whispered in her ear. He pulled off her boxer shorts as his hands slid down her legs. She let out a moan as they made their way to the inside of her thighs.

She arched up against him, pressing her hips into his erection. She moved her hips back and forth feeling his manhood rub against her. It sent shivers of desire through her body.

She took in his nude body. He was amazing. She felt little thrills of excitement where he touched her.   He eased her back down on the bed and ran his fingers along her body. As he teased her body with the gentlest of touches, the sensations became more than she could handle. She needed to feel him deep inside of her.

In one swift movement, he plunged deep inside of her, filling her completely. His rhythm became faster and more desperate with each thrust.

She felt the orgasm building as he thrust deeper into her. Her body shuddered as the sensations grew. He increased his speed, sending her further into pure delicious torture. He kept moving faster and faster against her climax, letting it continually build – orgasming over and over again.

Chapter 27

The next night, Melancon found herself unable to sleep and headed into the office early that morning. Since no one else was there, she grabbed the case files and headed into the conference room.

She settled into a chair and opened the files. She pulled out the pictures of the crime scene and skeletal remains. With the bodies having been found in the middle of the bayou, the killer was using a boat for transporting the bodies. That didn't help, though; just about every household here had a boat.

With it having been skeletal remains retrieved, there was no way to obtain a timeline as to when these poor souls were killed. It was impossible to work up an accurate timeline.

This guy needed privacy to dispose of these bodies, so he had to be doing it during the night. She reviewed the reports page by page. She examined every word and photograph meticulously, praying something jumped out at her.

Melancon was so engrossed in the files that she didn't hear Picou coming up behind her, "How long have you been here?"

"You scared the crap out of me. I can't get this case out of my mind." As he handed her a cup of coffee, she replied, "You are my hero."

He laughed, "I aim to please."

Chapter 28

He lay in his bed, staring up at the ceiling. The full moon spilled into the tiny room helping to push the shadows away. He needed God to talk to him. He needed to hear what his next mission was supposed to be, His reverent word.

He had grown tired of waiting for Mia to be his. He was ready to cherish and love her. He must complete his mission first. He needed to rid the impurities, immoralities and prurient behavior that plagued this town.

Unable to sleep, he rolled off the bed. As if drawn by a powerful magnet, he headed toward the kitchen. He was freezing. He had never believed in voodoo because it was against God's Christian beliefs, but right now he swore someone had cursed him.

He must have angered God as He was not talking to him tonight, helping to ease his troubled mind. The only way to appease him was to send him another soul to be cleansed. With so many sinners, who would it be this time?

Even though it was still in the early morning hours he decided to head to the boat and prepare for his day.   He planned to go out shrimping tonight, so he may as well use this time wisely. Plus, this gave him time to hunt before leaving.

***

It was only six o'clock in the morning, and it was already hot outside. She was ready for fall and the coolness that came with it. The way the leaves fell from the trees, it may not be much longer before the season was here. Sweat poured down her back. She still had five more pounds to lose before she was back to pre-baby weight and was determined to reach it before the holidays. Her family was finally accepting that she had a baby out of wedlock. Her parents even offered to watch the baby for her so that she could return to school.

She could smell the rain in the air. The rain clouds hung heavy, waiting to break free. She hoped she made it home before the rain fell. The fog was thick along the bayou, and it was hard to make out anything. All around her was complete emptiness.

The hairs on the back of Sally Dawson's neck prickled as she ran past the dock this morning. Her eyes scanned the area to see what brought this unwelcome chill. She looked over at the shrimp processing plant near the end of the dock and wondered if someone was over there. If you did not know that the plant was still in business, you would think it was a neglected building. The owner did not care about the broken windows or overgrown grounds. It had always given her the creeps, which was most likely causing her jittery nerves. From this distance, the building looked haunted, what with the windows having mismatched glass shards and plastic sheets taped up behind the broken glass. If the owner didn't want to replace shattered windows he could have at least knocked out the remaining shards of glass, she thought.

Chapter 29

Sally tried to figure out why she was so cold. Maybe the air conditioner was set too low. When she went to move, she hit her knee on a hard surface. She opened her eyes and found that complete darkness surrounded her. A blanket of ice covered her. Feeling around, she swore she was stuck inside a large ice chest.

She panicked. Now was not the time to be scared out of her mind. She forced herself to take deep breaths, and tried to relax. She needed to keep her wits about her and think if she wanted to escape. She attempted to force the ice chest open, but it wouldn't budge. As the cold seeped into her bones, she felt herself losing consciousness once again.

Her mind felt funny, as if she was hung over. As she forced herself to wake up, she couldn't put the pieces together. What happened to her? She had an uncomfortable feeling. Her head lolled back and forth as she continued to focus on her surroundings.

Sally slowly opened her eyes and saw nothing but darkness. She shut her eyes tight hoping to remove the sleep out of her eyes. When she opened them, total darkness still enveloped her. Maybe it was early. She looked at her alarm clock on the right only to find complete darkness. She tried to take in her surroundings. She was not in her room. Where was she? Fear jolted her system; she was awake now.

She remembered strong arms wrapping around her, forcing her to breathe into an old rag saturated with a drug. She remembered waking up covered in ice, but she was no longer cold. She must have been moved once again.

She tried to move her arms and realized her arms and legs were both restrained. She listened for any sounds that may tell her if anyone else was around, but silence greeted her. The odor of the room made her nauseous, from the smell she was probably on a shrimp boat. Funny how that smell didn't wake her up, how it was just now permeating her senses. By the gentle swaying of the room, she knew she was on a shrimp boat.

She tried to remember how she wound up here. The last thing she remembered was running down by the dock.

As panic set in, the surrounding darkness became oppressive and thick. The air grew heavy. Her breathing became labored.   She was having a panic attack. She must remain calm and rational, but it was hard to do under these circumstances. She had never liked the dark.

Then she saw a movement in the shadows. As he came closer, she cringed in fear. She knew this man, yet there was a sinister look about him that she'd never noticed before. His smile made her skin crawl. Whatever he had planned for her couldn't be good. If he had intended on letting her live, he would have hidden his face.

As he began his torture, she felt the blood oozing down her skin. She wasn't sure how much she lost, but it wasn't enough to kill her yet. He was still waiting for her to confess her sins. She wished she knew what sins to confess to, and she would do it to stop his toying with her. She was ready to die, to escape this unbearable pain.

***

He watched the light fade from her eyes. The life slowly left her body.

The thunderstorm came in hard and fast. It was pitch black outside. The rain came down in sheets as the thunder shook the cabin of the boat. He needed to make sure no one else was anchored nearby so he could dispose of her body. He prayed he didn't upset God. This one never confessed to her sins.

He said a quick prayer over her dead body, "In the name of the Father, the Son and the Holy Spirit I release you my child. Your soul shall soon be cleansed. Go in peace."

After ensuring no one was near, he tossed her over the bow of the boat and prayed God allowed her into his Kingdom.

Chapter 30

Picou was going over his files once more when his desk phone rang. "Picou."

"Detective, I have a concerned parent. Her daughter went out for a morning run, and hasn't come back home."

Picou dreaded hearing that they may have another missing woman, especially a younger woman. He waited as the dispatcher escorted the mom to his desk. He saw the baby in her arms and cringed.   "Detective Picou?"

"Yes, please have a seat."

Mrs. Dawson stated, "Sally went out for her usual morning run before school, but never came home." Forcing back the tears, she continued, "Detective, my daughter would never leave her son. He means the world to her."

Picou asked, "What about the baby's father? Are there any problems between Sally and him?"

"No, when he found out she was pregnant, he left. He joined the military and the last I heard he was stationed overseas."

Picou's brows knitted together. This scenario was turning out to be too commonplace around here. He needed to ascertain if this was a missing person's case or a young girl who suddenly decided to run away.

Mrs. Dawson handed him a photo, "Here is a photo of Sally."

Picou stared at the photo of Sally Dawson. She looked so young and innocent, a complete opposite to the women they suspected their serial killer hunted.

After Mrs. Dawson left, he called Detective Melancon. "We have another missing woman. Sally Dawson went for a run and didn't return home. I'm arranging a search party now."

"Damn, I don't like this. If it is our guy, he is escalating."

After hanging up with Melancon, he arranged the search team, "We will search the marshlands, walking trails and dock. Brent Comeaux with Wildlife and Fisheries is asking for volunteers also. We will search in a grid pattern to make sure nothing is missed."

After everyone was assigned a section to search they headed out. By lunchtime dread had settled heavy in Picou's gut, he told Melancon, "Alons pas! No luck today. All the search parties came up empty handed."

"I don't understand how she disappeared into thin air."

As the search party left, Picou wondered if they would ever know what happened to Sally Dawson, or even Misty Olivier. No one had heard from Misty since the night she disappeared.

Chapter 31

Michelle Guilliot checked into the hotel in New Orleans and let herself into the room. After making sure the door was locked, she spent a few moments leaning against it. She slowly relaxed.

Walking into the bathroom, she splashed cool water on her face. She couldn't believe she was back home. She had no idea where her baby sister was, but she feared she was in trouble or worse, something horrible had happened to her.

Michelle let out a deep sigh as her turbulent thoughts focused on her sister. She would find Caroline. Somehow trouble always found her sister, but she kept landing on her feet.

Caroline called her at least once a week, and it had been several weeks since she heard from her. They lived in different states now. Michelle wanted to move far from here, but Caroline refused to leave. Caroline never said how she made a living, but she suspected that it was something she would never to admit to. Caroline was always entertaining her with her crazy adventures and romantic affairs. The last few times they'd talked though, Caroline had sounded depressed. She talked paranoid, swearing someone was following her. She would catch a glimpse of a man lurking in the shadows. Caroline laughed it off, but Michelle had a feeling she was really frightened.

Caroline told Michelle one night she thought it might be an ex-boyfriend that had not taken their breakup well. When she didn't call her the first week, Michelle assumed she was busy. But it had been three weeks, and Michelle was fearful something happened to her.

Michelle called the New Orleans Police Department to report her sister missing, but they blew her off. Every day that passed and she didn't hear from Caroline, the more convinced she became that something bad happened to her.

The police had her information and assured her they would look into it, but she suspected they were just feeding her platitudes and reassurances. She didn't believe that they would even look into Caroline's disappearance. Not feeling comfortable with her sister missing, Michelle boarded a plane and headed south to Louisiana.

The next morning Michelle woke up early and put a pot of coffee on to brew. She had a long day ahead of her if she wanted to look for her sister and hopefully bail her out of whatever trouble she had gotten herself into. She would do anything for Caroline, including coming back here to search for her.

The aromatic smell of coffee filled the room. She hurriedly got dressed and headed out after pouring her a cup to go. She still had no idea where she wanted to start, but figured a good place would be the New Orleans Police Station.

As she headed out a local newspaper article caught her attention. She walked back over to the newspaper machine and had a hard time believing her eyes. The reporter wrote about bodies being found in a small town not far from here. A feeling of dread came over her. One of the unidentified bodies had been dead for approximately a month. As much as she hated to admit it, that fit in with her sister's disappearance. She searched her purse for fifty cents to purchase the paper. Once she got it, she read the story in further detail.

Without thinking twice about her decision, she knew she needed to head to Bear Corner and learn more about these bodies found. She would bring a picture of her sister along with the toothbrush and hairbrush she found in her small hotel room. Maybe if she provided them a DNA sample they would be able to help her out more. She prayed her gut feeling was wrong, and it was not her sister among the unidentified bodies there.

The sky rolled with a mass of gray clouds, and the air became thick with humidity. Michelle glanced anxiously at the ominous clouds. She didn't like the idea that she may have to drive back to New Orleans in the rain. Hopefully, the rain held off. Bayou roads were no place to be driving during a thunderstorm, especially if you were unfamiliar with the area.

It took longer to get to Bear Corner than she had expected. By the time she made it there her stomach was growling, reminding her she had missed breakfast and lunch. She slowed down and searched for a place to eat. An antique metal sign announcing Bear Corner Diner swung under the awning of the old building. The painted lettering on the old sign was fading. She pulled into an open parking space almost right in front of the small diner and hurried inside. Bells on the door jangled as she entered and the few patrons still there stopped what they were doing to see who walked in. She found a seat at the bar. A waitress came over with a menu and asked, "Can I get you something to drink sugar?"

"A coffee would be great."

"Coming right up."

Along with her coffee, the waitress handed her several packets of sugar and creamer. She breathed in the rich coffee aroma and added her usual two sugars and cream. "Would you like something to eat cher," the waitress asked.

Starving, she looked over the menu, "I'll take a shrimp po'boy."

While she waited for her food, Michelle thought about everything that had happened recently. She prayed that her sister's body wasn't among the bodies.

As she set her food in front of her, the waitress asked, "What brings you to the area?"

"My sister went missing in New Orleans."

"New Orleans is a bit away?"

"I saw the article about the missing bodies found here and I am worried that my sister may be among them."

"Mon Dieu! I hope dat's not true."

"So do I, but I haven't heard from her in a while, and I wanted to make sure."

"Well, cher, this may be your lucky day. You see dat man over at the end of the bar. Dat is Sheriff Riley. He would be the man dat you need to talk to."

Without waiting, the waitress called out, "Sheriff Riley, dis young woman needs to talk to you."

Michelle watched as the man sauntered over. He wasn't like the sheriffs she had met. He was tall with broad shoulders. The expression on his lean, tanned face was stern, almost brooding.

The way this man looked at her sent bolts of electricity pulsing through her body. There was something wickedly sexy about him. She swore the way he looked at her he could see right through her clothes. She forced herself to snap out of it. This was not the time to fantasize about a man. She was here to search for her sister.

"What can I help you with?" His voice was low and smoky, that Cajun accent of his sent shivers down her spine.

Her lungs seemed incapable of taking in air as she thought of the reason she was here. She tried to draw in a slow, deep breath to steady herself, and tilted her chin up. Her legs shook, and panic clawed its way up to the back of her throat. Tears pooled and swirled in her eyes, blurring her vision of the sheriff. "My sister went missing in New Orleans and I'm worried she may be one of the bodies found here."

He looked at her and watched as the tears formed in her eyes. "Well, now cher, don't cry. Just because she is missing doesn't mean she is dead."

"I hope that my gut feeling is wrong, but I know you have unidentified bodies here and I brought my sister's hairbrush and toothbrush."

Sheriff Riley looked at her, "Let's go to my office and talk about this a little more in private."

Michelle looked around and realized everyone in the diner was listening to their conversation. By the time she finished explaining her fears and reasoning behind them, most of the afternoon had passed.

Before leaving, Sheriff Riley took the hairbrush and toothbrush over to the coroner for him to do a DNA comparison. He explained to Michelle, "It is unlikely that we will get a match. I should warn you that it is not a quick process, it will take at least a week to get results back, possibly longer."

Michelle looked up at him, "I just couldn't sleep at night knowing I didn't do everything in my power to find my sister. She is the only family I have left. I have pored over her banking and phone records since the last time I heard from her. A few days after I talked with her, she dropped off the face of the earth. She has not accessed her bank account, used her debit card or used her phone in three weeks."

"You yourself said that she had talked about leaving New Orleans."

Michelle let out a deep breath, "I realize that my sister's occupation made her vulnerable to people with dubious backgrounds. Regardless of that fact Sheriff, I don't see her going this long without using her phone, even if she had a substantial amount of cash on her."

"Is there a way I can get in touch with you if I need to? Also, my detectives may have some follow-up questions or want to check out where your sister was last seen?"

Michelle wrote down her cell phone number and where her sister had been living recently. "I have gone over her hotel room with a fine tooth comb searching for something that would point me in her direction. They are more than welcome to go there. I paid the manager up front to keep the room available for the remainder of the month. I have a hotel room at The Riverside Plaza, but I may stay here for a few days."

***

Sheriff Riley doubted she would have any more luck staying here instead of New Orleans. If her sister wanted to disappear, then it would be hard for her to be found.

Sheriff Riley could see that guilt was tearing her apart, "You aren't planning on driving back to New Orleans tonight are you, cher?"

"I thought about it. Besides, I left most of my stuff in my hotel room."

"Why don't I find you a room here tonight? You look as if you are ready to drop."

"I'm fine. It's not that long of a drive."

"I know you are staying up at night worrying about your sister."

"I have, but sleeping here won't change that any." She gave him a wry smile, "I plan on talking to a few of her friend's tomorrow. After that maybe I'll come back here to see if you have found out anything."

He gave her a look of genuine concern, "You shouldn't talk to these people by yourself."

She bristled at that remark, "I don't need a babysitter. I went by myself the other day and was fine. Besides, I need you and your detectives working on identifying those bodies."

He was still concerned about her talking to her sister's "friends". It didn't take him long to figure out what Caroline's occupation may be from her address in New Orleans.

"How do you plan on talking to your sister's friends? They may suspect you are an undercover cop looking to make a bust."

"I plan on acting like a newbie working the corner. It may take a day or two before they open up, but I can't go home without answers."

Sheriff Riley stared at her in complete and utter disbelief. Of all the asinine things he had heard over the years, that may take the cake. "That is signing your death wish. All it takes is asking just one person the wrong question and you will be alligator food around there. It is best that you contact the N'Awlins Police Department."

She was shocked by his vehemence to her plan. "But…"

He continued to stare at her as if she had lost her mind. He interrupted her. "It is way too dangerous for you to ask questions down there. This is a different breed of people you plan on questioning. They would just as soon stab you in the back as talk to you."

***

She didn't understand why he was acting this way. He didn't even know her or what she was capable of. She had a way of putting people at ease, getting them to trust her and open up. She had always been good at this. Besides, if she didn't act on something as radical as this, she feared she would never find her sister. Despite Sheriff Riley's assurances, Michelle was convinced that something bad happened to her sister.

After promising Sheriff Riley that she wouldn't do anything crazy, she began the drive back to New Orleans. As she drove, she wondered what it would be like to be involved with him. He seemed so protective and caring. One look from the Sheriff's meltingly sexy eyes almost had her forgetting why she was here. She even considered staying in town to be near the handsome sheriff. But finding her sister was her top priority right now. If only she had met him under different circumstances. He had her dreaming of dancing the night away in his arms and making love all morning.

She forced herself to snap out of her daydream. The last thing she needed was to become romantically involved with a man.

When she returned to the hotel she had just enough time to take a shower and get dressed. She had stopped by a local clothing store earlier and picked up a short miniskirt and a royal blue tube top. She slipped on a pair of high stiletto heels and prayed she didn't break her neck while walking the streets. After one more inspection of herself in the mirror, she headed to Bourbon Street.

Chapter 32

Sheriff Riley had a gut feeling Michelle wouldn't heed his advice. So, he decided to follow her and make sure she didn't get herself into any trouble she couldn't handle. This woman was just as determined as a hungry alligator when it came to finding her sister. He couldn't think of a more insufferable woman he had ever met or a more beautiful one.

One look had him drawn to her. She had the bluest eyes and the face of an angel, with a mouth that begged to be kissed.

As he neared the hotel, he watched in disbelief as she headed to Bourbon Street. Michelle's outfit would land her in a heap of trouble. A multitude of blasphemies ran through his head as he followed her. She was liable to get them both shot, maybe even killed. *Quelle betise*! The little fool.

He couldn't believe that she was going through with this fool hearted plan. He should have known she would be too stubborn to listen to him. Why must women be so damned hard headed? He told her she shouldn't go through with this foolishness, and she should have listened to him. It was as simple as that.

Sheriff Riley watched her disappear into the mass of people. He strained to catch a glimpse of her outrageous outfit, but she seemed to blend in with the crowd. He, on the other hand, looked like a tourist.

Sheriff Riley watched the crowd. Another human being could melt into this group and just watch the ever-changing scene without being seen - unless you pissed off the wrong person. He had a feeling that Michelle was a person that could wear even a saint's nerves thin.

Unable to keep track of her at this distance he moved in closer. Following her was about to bring his blood pressure sky high. The inebriated crowd was getting rowdy. Several people were dancing in the street to the mixture of music that was playing. Several more working girls joined the crowd, attracting even more male onlookers. He couldn't believe Michelle was in the thick of this crowd.

He saw a young man approaching Michelle, and his hackles rose. He heard a low wolf call as the man moved in closer to her. He knew what this man had on his mind, and he had reservations as to whether or not Michelle understood what he might be interested in. Sheriff Riley had no doubt Michelle's sister knew how to handle this crowd, but did she?

He planned on keeping a very close eye on her. There was no reason to make any moves until needed, even though he wanted to rush in and save her. He wondered what it would be like to switch places with that guy. How good would it feel to dance with her, flirt with her, wrap his arms around her, and kiss her like he meant it?

Would she let him be a part of her life or did she see him as merely someone who could help find her sister? Would she allow him to take her to bed as a man and take her mind off of her problems? He wanted to feel those legs wrapped around him in the throes of passion, see desire for him in her eyes. He wondered if she was a tigress in bed.

Damn, it shouldn't bother him, but it was killing him to watch these men leer at her, pawing at her body. She was not a two bit whore they could offer money to and she gave them a glimpse of her flesh. Mon Dieu, she was a lady. He had to get a hold of himself. She was not his woman; it shouldn't matter to him that she wanted to put herself in harm's way.

Hell, she didn't even look as if it bothered her to show off her goods. Maybe she and her sister were more alike than he realized. It was just that she had such a look of innocence about her.

He watched as she moved her body to the music, laughing and carrying on with the crowd. She was lapping up the attention she received from men and women alike. He listened to her squeal in delight when a man lifted her up and swung her around. He was surprised at how well she treated these complete strangers. She talked to them as if they were old friends. She flirted easily with the men that surrounded her. Sheriff Riley clenched his fists and gritted his teeth as he watched her carry on like a complete fool.

In the next instant, he saw a look of fear in her eyes. He tried to catch her attention so she could break free of the crowd and run to him. Looking around to see where the danger lay he realized she was in no peril. She just had no idea that this was how they acted down here.

He could see the panic building in her face. Unaware of the fact that he was moving toward her, he pushed his way through the rowdy crowd. Suddenly he was by her side, pulling her into his arms.

* * *

Bourbon Street at night was not what Michelle expected, and she began to regret her plan. Maybe she should have listened to Sheriff Riley's advice.

The raucous street was teaming with an assortment of characters. People carrying brightly colored plastic and foam to-go cups filled with various alcoholic concoctions swarmed Bourbon Street like locusts. The crowd consisted of tourists and locals clad in as few clothes as they could get away with. Michelle was thankful that she at least didn't stick out like a sore thumb.

As Michelle walked into the crowd, she became overwhelmed with the heady scent of alcohol, heavy perfume and sweaty bodies, along with the other usual nightly smells that emitted from the surrounding businesses. The further down she traveled on Bourbon Street, the more pungent the smells became. The air was overwhelmed with the smell of food being fried and rotting garbage mixed in with the murky smell of the Mississippi River. Music blasted from the neighboring bars and restaurants lining the street. It was a melody of zydeco, jazz, blues, rock and no telling what else. She had no idea how people conversed out here.

As soon as the trouble started, she melted into Sheriff Riley's arms, never more glad to see this man before in her life. She was so thankful he had rescued her. She thought she could pull this off with no problems. What could be so hard about asking a few questions? It had been going well until a man grew tired of the partying and wanted her to go back to his room. He refused to take no for an answer.

She never suspected that saying no to a man could cause so many problems. To think he had expected her to take his money for, for – sex. She had her suspicions about what her sister did to make ends meet, but she never considered it in detail. Until that awful moment, she had believed the night was going fairly well.

He was holding her so close that she felt the suppressed anger in the tight muscles of his forearms. There was more anger there than she had expected. She couldn't understand why he was so livid with her. He barely knew her.

She heard Sheriff Riley mutter under his breath, "I need a drink, a big one."

As he was pushing her away, he looked down at her, "Don't ever do that again. What would you have done if I hadn't been here?"

Michelle shuddered at the thought. The look on his face told her he would make sure she didn't do anything this foolish again. "I have learned my lesson."

"Tres Bien."

They kept threading their way through the unruly crowd until they made it clear of Bourbon Street. Once they could hear themselves think he asked, "Well, did you at least learn anything from this little adventure of yours?"

She let out an exasperated sigh, "I learned that my sister was a popular girl. But no one has seen her in several weeks. No one could give me an exact date of when they last saw her."

Now that she had time to catch her breath, the sultriness of the night hit her. Looking up at him and seeing the concern in his eyes sent a quiver deep into the pit of her stomach. She took a deep breath. She could smell the Mississippi River, reminding her of the bodies that were tossed out like trash in the bayou.

She had forgotten what it was like to live down here. While some couldn't wait to leave the south during the summer months, not returning until the winter, she had always relished the summer days and nights. Something about the warmth and humidity calmed her. She had always been told that she was hot-blooded, if they only knew how true that statement was.

She sneaked a glance at Sheriff Riley. He was a complete opposite to the men she usually fell for. She fell for the handsome bad boys that broke her heart into a million little pieces. Not that Sheriff Riley wasn't attractive, mind you. In fact, this man was so damned sexy that she could see herself falling for him in a heartbeat.

When they made it back to her hotel, Sheriff Riley stopped at the main door, "Can I trust you to make it to your hotel room from here?"

She looked up at him, "You aren't planning on driving back at this hour?"

"Mais oui, I will take a cat nap in my truck and head back."

She looked at him incredulously, "You will do no such thing. You saved my life and the least I can do is offer you a place to sleep."

"Cher, I don't think that is such a good idea. I should go."

Her eyes beseeched him, "Please don't go. I don't want to be by myself tonight. If you are worried about where you will sleep, the room has two double beds. I promise I can keep my hands to myself." As she made the joke, she was grinning ear to ear.

***

Aw, hell. He had a weakness for a damsel in distress. She looked so pitiful right now that he couldn't find it in him to tell her no. Sometimes doing the right thing was hard. This would be one of those times.   But she was looking at him for support and compassion. He could never live with himself if something happened to her.

Letting out a sigh, he told her, "All right, I'll stay as long as it won't be an imposition."

Chapter 33

Sheriff Riley and Michelle went to breakfast before he had to head back to Bear Corner. Michelle still hadn't decided what she would do just yet. She wasn't ready to go back home without knowing what had become of her sister.

Maison du Café was busy this morning, but they managed to sequester an outside table that overlooked the Mississippi River on one side and the busy sidewalk on the other. The concierge at the hotel had recommended this place, stating that it was popular among the locals and the tourists. By the size of the crowd in here, he was correct.

She slipped on her sunglasses and perused the menu. "Everything looks so good."

The waitress stopped by their table, "Are y'all ready to order?"

Sheriff Riley grinned at the frazzled young waitress, "Morning cher, I would like the eggs benedict. Can we also have café au laits and an order of your bite size beignets?"

"Yes sir. And you miss?"

Michelle was still perusing the menu, "I'm not sure what to try." Glancing over the menu one more time, "I will have the mushroom and spinach omelet."

The waitress smiled at her, "That is very good. I'm sure you will enjoy it."

The waitress returned with their beignets and café au laits almost immediately. The tantalizing aroma made Michelle's mouth water. This was one of the things she missed about living down here. South Louisiana seemed to be the only place where you could get beignets. She popped one into her mouth and moaned in delight. They were so light and fluffy, almost melting in her mouth.

She noticed that Sheriff Riley was watching her eat, and gave him a wicked grin, "There is nothing like the food down here. Whenever I come this way I gain at least ten pounds."

Sheriff Riley asked Michelle, "What kind of job do you have that allows you to take off from work whenever you need to?"

"I design jewelry. I started out as a peon at a large company designing generic cookie cutter jewelry so to speak. It was a nice place to work, but they didn't allow me to branch out and create items that were more abstract, fearing they wouldn't sell. For them jewelry had to be mass produced. I managed my pennies and finally saved enough money to design jewelry at my house. When I had enough pieces designed to sell on the internet, I created a website and decided to see if I would get any hits. What started out as a small secondary business in my tiny spare bedroom soon took off. When the bigwigs at the company I worked for found out what I was doing on the side, they accused me of using their equipment. I proved that while there I did nothing but work on their jewelry, and they had no claim to mine. Once they realized how well I was doing and the talk my work was generating, they wanted me to start a line with them. But after everything they had put me through, I cut all ties with them. Besides, my business was picking up.”

Michelle realized she had been talking non-stop since they arrived. Sheriff Riley was much more patient than she would have guessed.

“I’m sorry. I didn’t mean to go on and on. My career is nowhere near as exciting as being a cop.”

Sheriff Riley gave her an indecipherable look, “You are one hell of an interesting woman. What are your plans now? Do you plan on going back home or are you staying in New Orleans?”

She shook her head, “I am staying, but don’t worry, I promise I won’t be as foolish as I was last night. I still want to talk to some of Caroline’s friends. I want to know if they can remember anything out of the ordinary. I can’t leave without knowing what happened to her. I can design my jewelry from here. That is the one good thing about my business; I can work from my laptop. When it comes to the actual making part of it, I have a company that helps me with that. Plus, I may be able to find some gemstones around here to work with. I can also visit the local jewelry stores to drum up some more businesses to carry my line.”

Sheriff Riley picked up a napkin and carefully wiped her lip, “You had a little sugar on your mouth.”

His innocent touch sent shock waves through her body, “Oh, thank you.” She felt the heat from embarrassment move up her face. She looked down at her clothes to make sure she wasn't covered in the sugar. As much as she loved beignets she had not figured out how to eat them without being covered in the sugary powder that coated the delectable treat.

***

Mais, quelle espece de tete dure, elle! Damn, obstinate woman. She was going to get herself killed looking for her sister. C'est fou, sa! It was crazy to stay here. If something bad had happened to her sister then whoever caused her harm did not want a nosy sister sniffing around. "It is too risky asking questions around here. What happens if you ask the wrong person the right question? What if that person had something to do with her disappearance?"

"Well then maybe the police will actually listen to me."

He'd never been so torn before. The cop in him wanted to see her go back home and far away from any danger she may place herself in. But the man in him wanted her to stay so that he could get to know her. There was something mysteriously intriguing about her.

He told her, "You are a damn stubborn woman."

She let out a laugh.

"Je t'amuse? Did I say something to amuse you?"

"I have been told that I can be very willful. It drove my mother and sister nuts when I refused to back down from something."

Now it was his turn to laugh. This woman was irresistible.
He couldn't explain why, but he wanted her.

Chapter 34

A week later, Dr. Harrison called with his findings. "Sheriff Riley we have the DNA results back on the floating Jane Doe and the sample Ms. Michelle Guilliot provided. They are a match."

Damn, Sheriff Riley thought to himself. Michelle had decided four days ago to stay over at Cajun Cabins. She wanted to be here when the DNA results came back, and he dreaded breaking the news to her. He assumed that she was just an overwrought sister, but now he had to confirm her suspicions.

He hoped that by identifying one of the victims it may help to find the monster killing these women.

***

Michelle was surprised to see Sheriff Riley this early in the morning, "Sheriff Riley I wasn't expecting you. Come on in. I just put a pot of coffee on and was going to work a bit."

"Michelle, why don't you sit down? We need to talk."

Michelle felt an overwhelming sense of dread come over her, "It's about Caroline isn't it?"

He took Michelle's hand in his, "I am so sorry. Dr. Harrison confirmed that your sister was the unidentified victim."

Michelle felt as if her world was coming to an end. She had feared this day would come, but now that it was here she didn't know how to handle the news. She felt Sheriff Riley's strong arms pull her into him, but it didn't register. "Why? Why her?" She asked repeatedly through the sobs that racked her body.

"We are doing our best to capture this guy."

Grief stricken, "Nobody wanted to listen to me when she disappeared. Maybe if they had, she would still be alive."

***

Sheriff Riley wondered the same thing. If the New Orleans detectives had looked into this missing person report would they have discovered that several other women may have disappeared as well? There was only one way to confirm his suspicions and that was to go to New Orleans and talk to some of the "workers". They may have noticed a significant amount of their friends vanishing. These girls usually formed a tight bond on the streets, knowing they were the only ones who would band together in a difficult situation.

"I know you don't like to think about what your sister did for a living, but did she talk about a particular friend that may be able to answer some questions."

"I already asked those girls questions and they told me everything they knew."

Sheriff Riley looked into her eyes, "You asked about Caroline's disappearance. I plan on finding out if they were concerned about any others."

An understanding of what he was saying flashed across Michelle's face, "You think he has been doing this for a while don't you?"

"Your sister's body wasn't the only one found. Several skeletal remains were found. And yes, I suspect he has been at this for a while."

Sheriff Riley hated leaving Michelle by herself, but he wanted to get Picou and Melancon working on this angle right away. He told Michelle, "If you need anything at all, please call me. I'll come right over."

"I want to go with you to New Orleans."

"I don't think that's a good idea. Anyway, I plan on sending two detectives to talk to several people there."

She asked, "But won't they make them out for cops?"

"This time it won't matter. When word gets around that Melancon and Picou want to help them it will spread like wildfire. They just have to ask the right people the right questions."

"Please find this guy and make him pay for killing my sister."

***

Michelle couldn't believe her suspicions were right. She had never been this depressed. If Caroline had been killed in a car accident or by a terminal illness, it might have been easier to deal with her death. She knew life was short and that everyone must die, but this was different. Her sister's life was stolen from her by a monster. She worried that she would never fully recover from her sister's violent death.

What she wanted was for Sheriff Riley and his detectives to catch this bastard and make him fry.

Before she could head home, she had to plan her sister's funeral. How was she going to do this? She had to find out when they would release the body. Michelle didn't even know who would come to a funeral for her sister. They didn't have any family left. It was just her and Caroline, and now she was all alone.   Maybe she should consider a cremation and spread her ashes along Bourbon Street or the bayou.

Chapter 35

Sheriff Riley called Melancon and Picou into his office, "Don't get too comfortable, you both need to get ready to head to New Orleans."

Picou had been dreading this. He feared they were going to ask the FBI for help, "What's in New Orleans?"

"I have a possible lead."

Now Picou's interest was piqued. He was not expecting this news, "Did we get a tip that I don't know about."

Sheriff Riley informed them, "We got an ID on the floating Jane Doe. She was a working girl from New Orleans."

Melancon groaned, "None of those girls will talk to us."

"They will when you tell them the reason you are there. You want to ask them if they have noticed any disappearances over the last few months, possibly years. We have no idea how long this killer has been drowning his victims, but the sheer number of skeletal remains discovered is shocking."

Picou, "We can do that, sir."

As Picou and Melancon headed out for New Orleans, Picou hoped to learn some information that may lead to an arrest. Time was of the essence. At any moment, their killer could kidnap and murder another woman and if someone in New Orleans could give them any information this trip would be worth it.

Chapter 36

Mia had a difficult time getting things to come into focus. She was still nauseous from whatever he used to knock her out with. She tried to recall the last thing she could remember.

She had been surprised to find him standing there when she answered the door. She couldn't remember the last time she had talked to him. It was probably before she graduated high school. She remembered the rag he put over her mouth and the sweet smell. She tried not to breathe it in, but he held her with such force she didn't have a choice. She blacked out almost immediately.

She couldn't believe he may be the one responsible for murdering these people. She had a hard time understanding why.

She heard him enter the room, "Good, you're awake. I'm sorry I had to drug you. I didn't want to but I couldn't take the chance that you wouldn't hear me out."

"Why? Why are you doing this? Why did you kill all those innocent people?"

He looked at her as if she should already know the answer to that question, "The world around you was impure. I needed to cleanse the sinners' souls."

"Those people didn't know me. How did killing them help my world?"

He glared at her with an intensity that chilled her to her core. "Those people needed to be set free from everlasting damnation. They were sinners! They needed to be cleansed so they could be saved. I did this for you. I didn't want your world tainted with their evil ways. God personally selected me to do this mission. My plan was to surprise you when you were living in New Orleans, but when you saw me, you screamed and your neighbor called the police. I knew they wouldn't understand why I was there, and then God told me it was for the best, that my work was not done yet."

She stared at him in disbelief, "That was you in my apartment?"

"Yes. I didn't mean to scare you, but I was ready to be a part of your life. I never thought you would move back home, and I was surprised when you did. But God told me I had to finish ridding the world of sinners before I could make you mine. I couldn't wait to finish eradicating the world of sinners though, there are just too many. I need to have you; I can't wait any longer."

She couldn't believe what he was telling her, "Are you truly so demented that you think I am glad you are killing people?"

He yelled at her, spittle flying from his mouth. "I did this for you - so we could be together!"

She exclaimed, "You murdered innocent people!"

"Death was the only way to set their souls free."

Mia could see the anger flaring in his eyes, and she regretted upsetting him. His face contorted, becoming almost monster like. Maybe she should have coddled him. She just couldn't accept that he killed people for her. It was terrifying to watch him switch moods so quickly. One minute he was calm and the next he had the look of the devil about him.

"You need to let me go. People will wonder where I am."

A demonic laugh erupted from his chest. "They won't find you. Your boyfriend can't even figure out that I am the one responsible for setting these sinners free."

"Don't underestimate him. He'll find out who you are and come rescue me. He's smarter than you are. You are just a psycho with a few too many screws loose."

She realized that she had gone too far. He was furious with her. Moving quickly, he lifted her into the air as his hand closed around her throat. With her hands restrained behind her, she couldn't fight him. She gasped for air as his hand gripped her throat even tighter.

He let her go, dropping her to the floor unmercifully. No sooner than she hit the ground, his shoe connected with her stomach, sending an intense sharp pain throughout her body. As he stomped on her right leg, she heard the sound of bone breaking and the agonizing pain became unbearable. This man in front of her was stark raving mad. Slipping into unconsciousness, she heard him saying, "You are mine now. You belong to me. I can't allow you to leave me, ever!"

***

Chad heard his phone ringing and noticed the bakery's phone number on the caller id, "Miss me already."

"Chad, it's Shelly. I take it that Mia isn't with you then."

Apprehension built in his gut, "No, she was getting ready to head to the bakery when I left this morning. She mentioned needing to pay some bills before heading out. She's not there?"

"No, she usually opens up for me, but she hasn't shown up yet. I don't mind handling the shop, but it is really busy this morning. Plus, I'm getting worried about her. It's not like Mia not to call if she plans on being late. I tried her cell phone, but it went to voice mail."

Chad didn't like the sound of this. "I'm going to her house right now. I'll let you know what I find out."

When Chad arrived at Mia's house, he noticed her car was still in the driveway. He was terrified of what he may find in her house. He could not dismiss the possibility that Mia may be injured or even worse.

He knocked on the door, but there was no answer. Trying the handle, it was still locked from when he left this morning. He tried her cell phone one more time, but there was no answer. He was getting worried. He walked to the backyard, and the back door was also locked. Worried that something had happened to Mia, he broke the window in the back door and let himself in. He called out, "Mia, I'm sorry about the window. I'll have it fixed."

The house remained eerily silent. Cupping both hands around his mouth, he yelled, "Mia? Mia, come on, this isn't funny." He clung to hope that he would find her in the bathroom getting ready for work. The further he looked around, hope quickly vanished that Mia was somewhere inside safe and sound.   His eyes were misty and throat tight as he thought about the possibility that Mia had been abducted.   *Where could she be?*

As he continued to search the house; there was no sign of her or a struggle. He proceeded carefully though, not wanting to contaminate the scene. He would have forensics comb the house in case there were fingerprints they could lift. He felt like an intruder. It didn't matter that he had been in her house numerous times, right now he felt as if he was an uninvited guest peeking in on Mia. It was almost as if he was desecrating her private domain. For several minutes, he just stared out the kitchen window. He didn't even notice the activity on the bayou. Then it dawned on him, what if the intruder came in from the bayou and left the same way. He rushed down to the marsh to see if he noticed anything unusual. He saw that the reeds were crushed at the bank of the bayou, almost as if a small boat had been pushed ashore. He had to get forensics out here.

Panic set in. He didn't know what he would do without Mia. He loved being around her, the smell of her hair, the feel of her body pressed against his.

As the realization that the serial killer may have abducted Mia set in, he became paralyzed with fear. His phone ringing snapped him out of it. It was Sheriff Riley, "I take it she isn't at home."

Letting out an exasperated sigh, "No, sir. We need to get forensics here ASAP. I want the entire house dusted for prints. Also, it looks as if the abductor may have come in through the bayou. I want this checked out too."

"Don't worry son, we will find her. We have every officer and detective working on this case. I will have forensics out there pronto and we'll put a rush on any evidence we find. Do you have any leads?"

"Nothing definite yet. Jo and I were following up on some information we got from Caroline Guilliot's friends in New Orleans. Turns out you were right. Several women have turned up missing. They said that it could be weeks at a time before another one disappeared, sometimes almost a month. Jo and I believe we are looking at an oil rig worker. That would fit the timeline. One girl saw a man standing in the shadows, not approaching anyone but just staring. She also mentioned that he drove an older Dodge truck and when she walked by him he smelled. I asked her to meet with a sketch artist and one went up today to talk with her. Hopefully he will be back soon."

Sheriff Riley asked, "So you think Mia's disappearance has something to do with the killer?"

Picou was considering this possibility ever since Shelly called him. What was the chance that another person abducted Mia? "It is a bizarre coincidence, but Mia doesn't fit the killer's profile. I hope he isn't evolving."

Sheriff Riley gave further instructions to Picou, "I want you and Melancon to keep me informed every hour on the hour.

I don't care if it is just to say no leads. I want to make sure y'all are okay."

Picou stated, "Yes, sir, understood. Please let me know as soon as the sketch artist arrives."

"I will call you immediately.   Now if you need anything, don't hesitate to ask. Let's catch this bastard."

Picou hoped that the sketch artist hurried back. He wanted to waste as little precious time as possible. Each second was crucial if they were going to find Mia alive. He was terrified of what may happen to her if they didn't find out who this maniac was.

Picou didn't want to think about what Mia may be going through at this minute. He had to think like a cop and not a lover. Usually abductors started out by antagonizing their victims first. Crazed killers loved to taunt and tease like a cat with a mouse before moving in for the kill. They derived just as much pleasure from psychological torture as they did physical.

If Mia had any hopes of survival, she needed to keep her feelings under tight control and not let fear take over.

Picou was at the police station when the sketch artist arrived at the precinct. Forensics had already finished at Mia's house, finding nothing that would help them locate her.

Sheriff Riley and Detectives Melancon and Picou studied the picture. Sheriff Riley informed them, "I'll be damned, it's Carl Ledet. There is no doubt about it either. He fits your profile too. He runs his shrimp boat whenever he isn't working offshore. If he's not shrimping, then he's crabbing or fishing. He lives alone in his mom's parents' old house. They died several years back and left it to him. Carl is a loner, keeps to himself. Your informant is right - he's a big, burly man."

Picou was anxious to get out the door and rescue Mia, "What's his address."

"1526 Bayou Road." Putting his hand on Picou's shoulder, he informed him, "Let's do this right son. We don't want to go over there half cocked."

"Sheriff, if he has her, we don't know how long before he plans on killing her. He may already have. I've got to get over there."

Sheriff Riley instructed him, "Son, it won't take us anytime to get you back up over there. You and Jo head out, backup and ambulances will be right behind you. I will contact the Coast Guard just in case his shrimp boat is already on the water."

Picou felt the dread building in his gut. He hoped the boat was still at the dock. If he was out on the water, then Mia's chance of survival was grim.

It took less than fifteen minutes to make it to Carl Ledet's house. It looked like the other century old houses in the area, most of which hadn't seen fresh paint or repairs in a decade. The original asbestos shingles still hung on the sides of the house, severely weathered and peeling paint lined the outside of the house. Several shingles were missing, showing the black tar paper underneath. There were mature oak trees outlining the property with cedar and cypress trees lining the back.

Carl didn't care for lawn maintenance, and it looked like his neighbors shared the same sentiment. The lawns were overrun with weeds and dandelions. There were thistle bushes almost four feet tall in some areas. In the back of the house at the old dock sat the shrimp boat. He said a quick novena that Mia was okay. They had to split up, not knowing if Carl was on the boat or in the house. Melancon and her team would take the house and Picou would take the boat.

With warrant in hand, Melancon and Picou checked their weapons one more time before forcing their way in. They didn't want to give Chad the chance to run. The element of surprise was always a great advantage in this type of situation. They did not want to give him the chance to kill Mia, if she was still alive, before she could be rescued.

His gut clenched as the intense Louisiana sun beat down on his neck. A fine mist rose from the water as they made their way to the boat. The dank smell of the bayou permeated his senses. Apprehension grew deep inside him the closer he got to the boat, unsure of what he would find.

Chapter 37

Mia slowly opened her eyes. She tried to move, but the pain shooting through her body was excruciating, causing her to scream out.

Menace dripped from his tongue as he spoke to her, "Good, you're awake. This time you need to be nicer to me. I hate hurting you, but you didn't give me much of a choice."

He walked closer to her and kneeled down beside her, pulling her into his arms. Just the touch of him made her cringe. A wry smirk fell on his lips. "I have been waiting a long time for you to be mine. I have asked God to forgive you for sinning, giving your body to another while unwed. Soon you will realize my love for you is more than your detective friend's. You will come to love me just as much as I love you. It may take time, but I promise I will be patient."

He leaned in closer to her and kissed her forehead. She saw this as a chance to escape. She pulled her head back and slammed forward with every ounce she could muster. Blood poured from his nose and he yelped in pain. Even though her head hurt, she got up off the ground and charged him one more time, sending him crashing to the floor. She made a run for the door, ignoring the pain in her leg. Before she knew it, he grabbed her leg, twisting it with great force and pulled her back down.

***

Rage boiled in his gut. Like a slow moving tide, darkness fell over his eyes. He didn't like when he went to this place. He had been here before and every time he lost control. If he didn't snap out of it God's mission would be for naught. He would be manipulated by the demonic force. If this happened, Mia's life would come to a brutal end. He couldn't let that happen. He had waited too long for her to be his. Desperately he tried to reign in his anger. "You bitch. I can't believe you did that. You will pay for this."

She kicked at him with her good leg, trying to break free, "Let me go. You are sick. You will rot in hell for what you have done."

He picked her up and threw her like a rag doll. She landed hard against the wall. "Why must you make me hurt you? I have loved you for so long and have waited for this day. Why can't you accept my love? We are meant to be together, God told me so. Those women were harlots. They sold their bodies to men, tempting them with their wiles."

The anger still boiled inside of him. He squeezed his eyes shut and prayed. He asked God to strike down Satan's grip on him, to help him complete His mission. He prayed that God would banish this demon from his soul, freeing him from its evil force.

Suddenly, his face became eerily calm. The darkness faded from his eyes. His prayers worked. God had banished the evil from his soul. He left the room, slamming the door closed behind him.

***

Mia prayed that Shelly had called Chad when she wasn't there to open the bakery. She was confident in Chad's capabilities. She couldn't think of anyone else she would rather have looking for her.

Mia was still dazed from being thrown against the wall. Looking around, she tried to find a way to escape. If only she could get out of these bindings. She looked for something sharp to rub the tape over and noticed the corner of the table. It was rough and may just work. She scooted her way over to the table and forced herself to stand up. After a while she felt the duct tape loosening. It took a little bit of effort, but she finally freed her wrists.

She forced herself to remain standing, fighting against the pain in her broken leg. Catching herself on the corner of the table, she told herself she could do this. The pain was unspeakable, but she forced herself to move towards the door. She tried the doorknob only to find it locked. Her hopes were crushed. She feared she would never make it out of this hell hole. At first she thought the swaying of the room was from the drugs, but now she feared she was on a boat. Even if she managed to get out of here how would she get off a boat? She couldn't tell if they were moving or at the dock. She listened to see if the motors were running.

She pressed her ear up against the door and heard footsteps approaching. Maybe she could catch him off guard and lock him up in this room. She laid back down and acted as if she was still unconscious.

He slowly opened the door and stepped inside the room. Acting quickly she lunged towards him, catching him off guard. With all her strength, she pushed him to the floor and tried to make a run for it. As soon as she made it out of the little room, she locked the door. She heard him screaming her name and pushing against the small door. It wouldn't take long for him to break free from the room. Her broken leg slowed her down more than she liked. With each step the pain became worse.

As she went up the stairs leading out of the small cuddy cabin her captor grabbed her. She tried to squirm free, "Please. Please. Please. Let me go!"

He spun her around and slammed her body against the metal steps. She didn't feel the knife slide into her abdomen. Her body sagged forward into his waiting arms. He drug her back into the tiny room.

"Why must you disobey me? We will be happy together. I will be the perfect lover and husband. No one will ever love you as much as I do." He whispered in her ear. The feel of his hot breath against her skin nauseated her.

She felt the blood oozing down her side. She never even felt him stab her. Her body went into shock as her body grew cold.

For a moment she thought she heard footsteps on the deck. Her mind must be playing tricks on her. She felt him drop her roughly on the table and mutter something under his breath. She had a hard time staying awake. She felt the knife at her neck and knew he was getting ready to kill her.

***

When Picou stepped on the boat he heard Carl talking to someone. Relief flooded through his body, Mia must still be alive. He readied his Glock, taking off the safety as he walked downstairs.

"Let her go Carl."

"Don't take another step closer or I swear I'll kill her. If I can't have her then no one can."

Mia slumped forward, unable to stay alert. Looking at her, Chad was worried she may have lost too much blood. He feared they didn't get here soon enough to save her from this psycho, "Put the knife down Carl."

"That's not going to happen and we both know it. You will have to shoot me first. The question is can you take the chance that I won't kill her before you get the chance to kill me?"

"I don't want to kill you Carl. You are the only one who can help us identify the people you have murdered."

Carl pushed the knife closer to Mia's throat; a thin bead of blood drew from the contact with the tip of the knife. "Carl you need to let her go now."

Chad noticed the fury in his eyes. His rage was so intense that his eyes were out of focus. He moved as if a madman had taken over his body. "How dare you tell me what to do?" Without thinking he waved the knife wildly in all different directions.

The time had come to act with no second thoughts or regret. From the sound of Carl's wild voice he knew all reasoning in dealing with him was gone. Without hesitation Chad fired his gun, hitting Carl between the eyes. "Tell the paramedics to get down here now. She has lost a lot of blood.”

Chad pulled her into his arms, “Honey, can you hear me? The paramedics are on their way. Please stay with me . Mia, don’t you dare die on me. I can’t lose you now. Think of me and your family, how much we all love you.”

Chad moved out of the paramedics’ way so they could tend to her injuries. One was busy taking her vitals as the other started her on fluids. One of the paramedics confirmed what Chad feared, “She’s lost a lot of blood.”

“We’re losing her; we need to get her to the hospital now.”

Moving quickly, Chad scooped her up in his arms as one of the paramedics held the IV bag. With them being on a boat, they could not get the stretcher on board. Carefully stepping off the shrimp boat, he placed her on the stretcher waiting for them on the dock. “Let’s get her in the ambulance.”

The other paramedic put his hand on Chad’s shoulder, “Sir, you have to stay here. You can meet us at the hospital, but we need to work on her.”

He just nodded his head. His partner, Detective Jo Melancon, followed behind the ambulance. He stared at the blood on his hands. It was Mia’s blood and he could not get the vision of her lifeless body out of his mind. He had to accept the fact that she would not make it, but he continued to pray that she did. He couldn’t lose her now that he had found her. He prayed that she had enough fight left in her body.

Chapter 38

It sickened Sheriff Riley that someone from Bear Corner had
been killing women right under his nose. With Carl Ledet
dead they might never know the names of his victims, or
what happened to Misty Olivier and Sally Dawson. Dr.
Bendell and his team were working on identifying the
bodies but so far they had had no luck.

A thorough inspection of the boat and house uncovered a
journal of sorts that he had kept over the years. There were
over one hundred entries of "souls having been cleansed".

Sheriff Riley prayed that there weren't one hundred bodies
lying in a watery grave. Unfortunately, it was unlikely that
they would recover any more bodies than they already had.
The divers hadn't found any more remains and it would take
too much manpower to continue the search.

According to the journals these women were who he
considered sinners, mainly prostitutes who walked the
streets of New Orleans. He focused mainly on women who
wouldn't be missed if they disappeared. That was except
for Caroline Guilliot's sister. Because of Michelle's
unrelenting insistence, DNA results acknowledged her worst
fears; the unidentified body found floating in the bayou was
that of her sister.

Michelle chose to cremate her sister and scatter her ashes
along the marsh land. She also decided to rent a house
here and work from Bear Corner for a while, hoping to
come to terms with her sister's violent and tragic death.

And then there were the recent disappearances here of Misty Olivier and Sally Dawson. Their families may never know what happened to them.

Chapter 39

The beep of the heart monitor echoed in the hospital room. The shuffle of feet beyond the room, muffled voices and the clatter of rolling carts went unnoticed by him. Chad hadn't been able to move from this spot since he was allowed in the room. Outside, dawn was breaking. The sky was a mirage of colors, pink and lavender clouds mixed with the slate gray haze that loomed overhead. The weather matched his mood. The rain fell nonstop for the last several hours. He ran his hands through his hair as he stared at the small figure lying in the bed.

Mia still hadn't woken. The doctor informed him that they had her stabilized for now, but she wasn't out of the woods yet. Carl Ledet had done a number on her body.

Fear coursed through his body at the realization that he may still lose her. She looked so small and frail in the hospital bed. Her pale face looked ashen against the heavy bruises peeking out from under the bandages. Her hair lay lackluster against the pillow. He hated seeing the IV's and tubes that were going into her body. He tucked the blanket around her small frame, needing to touch her.

Anxiety and worry clawed their way through him. He couldn't help but pace the small room, worried about what was to come. He had been begging her to open her eyes, to move just one finger. His demands had been met with no response. He had been praying to God to let her live, but so far none of his prayers had been answered and she had not moved. Her heart beat was still slow but he was thankful that it was still beating.

The doctors informed him there was nothing more that they could do. It was in God's hands now. All anyone could do was wait for her to respond. Chad had never been a patient man, though. He couldn't stand waiting.

Throughout the night nurses came and went, taking her vital signs, checking her blood pressure, and making sure the IV fluids were as they should be. Still Mia never opened her eyes.

Sheriff Riley, Jo, and Mia's parents all tried to get him to go home, but he refused. He could not leave her side. Mia's mom allowed him to stay with her and he was thankful for that. She had not left the bedside either. She had been right here the whole time.

Chad had lost count of how many times he had prayed, but he bent his head one more time hoping this would be the prayer answered.

Chapter 40

Chad did not sleep well again last night. He couldn't remember the last good night's sleep he had had. Every time he closed his eyes, he saw Mia's lifeless body in his arms. That fateful night kept replaying in his mind. He continuously relived that horrific moment of seeing her lying there in her own pool of blood. If only they had put together the clues sooner.

It brought him little comfort knowing that Carl Ledet was dead. He reached over and brought her body closer to him. Feeling her lying next to him was the only thing that helped ease the hate away. He could never erase that atrocious night out of his mind, but he breathed a little easier knowing she was here with him. He didn't know if he would ever be able to let her out of his sight.

He still remembered walking into the hospital waiting to hear if she had died in the ambulance on her way in. His world came crashing down on him when he heard the ER doctor say she was flat lining, but Mia had enough fight left in her. After finding the knife had nicked her spleen, she was rushed into surgery.

That was the worst experience he had ever had to live through. And he hoped he never went through anything like that again. As soon as the surgeon came in the waiting room and told them Mia was critical but stable, Chad went out and purchased an engagement ring. He knew he could not live without her in his life.

Mia was in the hospital for over a week. She complied with her parents' wishes and moved in with them for a few weeks to recover. The night she moved back to her house he proposed. They married a month later, neither wanting to waste any more time. They both learned the hard way just how short life was.

Chad couldn't be happier. He was getting a chance to spend the rest of his life with the woman he loved and maybe someday they would welcome a baby into this world. Right now he was just happy to enjoy this time with his new wife.

Thank you!

Dear Reader,

Thank you for purchasing this book. I hope you enjoyed reading this novel as much as I enjoyed writing it.

It is very important for me to hear what you think about the book. Your reviews give me inspiration in my future writings. You can leave a review on Amazon, Goodreads or Barnes and Noble.

Your thoughts and opinions mean a lot to me.

Please enjoy a sample of 7 Deadly Sins. Another killer is stalking the streets of Bear Corner, Louisiana. He must save the town from the wicked. The first of the seven sinners, Pride, has been cleansed of her sins. He has six more to go before his mission is complete.

Also, be sure to check out my website and social media sites for upcoming books and giveaways.

Sincerely,

Mary Theriot

Links
Website www.maryreasontheriot.com
Goodreads for reviews -
http://www.goodreads.com/MaryReasonTheriot
Facebook, - http://goo.gl/Sd0VgY
Twitter - @Mktheriot
Google+ - +MaryTheriot
YouTube - http://goo.gl/ErM1M6
Pinterest - http://www.pinterest.com/mktheriot
Blog Page - www.maryreasontheriot.me

7 Deadly Sins

By: Mary Reason Theriot

Prologue

He dropped the knife into the sink. This was not just any knife, though.   This knife had set a soul free earlier in the evening. It was sharp enough to cut through steel. He watched in fascination as the blood of the sinner mixed with the water as he washed his hands. He had completed the first part of God's mission. His mother's soul was one-step closer to gaining entrance into the Kingdom of God. When his mother was diagnosed with cancer, he promised her they would defeat it. Not only had he failed to keep his promise, but he had let her commit the ultimate sin, suicide. The church denied his request to allow her body to pass through because she had committed such a grievous mortal sin.

That night he begged God to help his mother's soul find everlasting peace. There had to be a way for their heavenly Father to forgive his mother! That was when God came to him with a mission, eradicate the sinners and he would allow his mother eternal rest in heaven. Only after these sinners had atoned for their sins would his mother gain entry into His kingdom. Each day that her soul remained confined in purgatory was a day of unrest for him.

Earlier tonight, he saved this town from one of the wicked. This evening he cleansed Pride, the first of the seven sinners, of her sins.

Once he finished cleaning his hands, he moved onto the knife. The water in the sink was now a crimson red. He closed his eyes and visualized setting her soul free. He laid the knife on the counter to dry. He would return it to his arsenal of tools after his shower.

He placed his dark clothes in a black plastic trash bag for disposal; there was no sense in washing them. When he was preparing to begin God's mission, he purchased several disposable outfits from a thrift store in New Orleans. He knew the importance of disposing of any evidence as soon as he released a soul. He could not take the chance of the police stopping him just yet. First, he must complete his mission so God could forgive his mother and free her soul from Purgatory.

He headed to the bathroom and turned on the shower. Soon steam filled the room. He stepped into the shower and let the hot water run over him. He lathered the soap on his body over and over again until the water ran clear.

He dressed in dark clothes once again. By daybreak, this town would know what happened to sinners.

Chapter 1
Pride

Detective Chad Picou had not once regretted transferring from Baton Rouge, Louisiana to Bear Corner. He had felt welcomed here since the minute he moved into his house. He had never experienced such hospitality. Several of his neighbors even brought over little gift baskets and homemade goodies.

He also found out that he fit right in with the locals. When he moved here, he feared that he would miss the hustle and bustle of the city, but he preferred this small town way of life. He was comfortable in this small town and loved the people. Living in Bear Corner had also brought him closer to his Cajun heritage.

His duties as a detective could be mundane at times. Nothing much went on in the sleepy town, that was until storm waters revealed Carl Ledet's deadly secret earlier that year. Picou could finally close his eyes and not see Ledet holding that knife to Mia. His blood ran cold at the mere thought of what she had endured at the hands of that man. The only good thing that came from the experience involving Ledet was that it brought them even closer together.

Mia was the best thing that ever happened to him. She was the first woman he envisioned himself growing old with, which was why he married her.

Available in eBook and Paperback